THE
FAMILY DIAMOND

Also by Edward Schwarzschild
Responsible Men

THE
FAMILY DIAMOND

stories by

EDWARD SCHWARZSCHILD

ALGONQUIN BOOKS OF CHAPEL HILL   2007

Published by
ALGONQUIN BOOKS OF CHAPEL HILL
Post Office Box 2225
Chapel Hill, North Carolina 27515-2225

a division of
Workman Publishing
225 Varick Street
New York, New York 10014

Stories in this collection originally appeared, in very different form, in the following publications: "Open Heart" in *River Styx*, "No Rest for the Middleman" in *Moment Magazine*, "Distance Man" in *Southwest Review*, "Proposals and Advice" in *The Virginia Quarterly Review*, and "What to Expect" in *FiveChapters.com*.

Printed in the United States of America.
Published simultaneously in Canada by Thomas Allen & Son Limited.
Design by Anne Winslow.

This is a work of fiction. While, as in all fiction, the literary perceptions and insights are based on experience, all names, characters, places, and incidents either are products of the author's imagination or are used fictitiously. That said, however, it's true that Milly and Charlie are much less imaginary and fictitious than everyone else in the book.

Library of Congress Cataloging-in-Publication Data
  Schwarzschild, Edward, 1964–
    The family Diamond: stories / by Edward Schwarzschild.—1st ed.
      p. cm.
    ISBN 978-1-56512-410-3
    1. Jewish families—Fiction.   2. Philadelphia (Pa.)—Fiction.
    3. Short stories, Jewish.   4. Domestic fiction, American.   I. Title.
    PS3619.C489F36 2007
    813'.6—dc22   2007007968

10 9 8 7 6 5 4 3 2 1
First Edition

For my mother and her father.
And in memory of Mildred D. Merin.

In Boston they ask, how much does he know?
In New York, how much is he worth?
In Philadelphia, who were his parents?

—MARK TWAIN

CONTENTS

Open Heart

I.

The *bubba* of this story, Mrs. Mildred Diamond, had only one working eye, and she had an artificial hip that made her "oof" out loud and sway with each step, but she could still look around for herself, and she knew that the place where the stern surgeon's assistant had told her to wait was no sunroom, and it would never be one, not in her lifetime. "We call this place 'the Sunroom,'" the assistant had proudly said, and it was all Milly could do to stop herself from saying, "Well, you can call it whatever you like, dear, but that doesn't change what it is."

In fact, it was not a room at all—it was a sixth-floor hallway that connected surgery and intensive care, bridging two hospital buildings. In this space, Milly sat and waited between visits with her husband, Mr. Charles Diamond, the *zayde* of this story. At age seventy-four, he was about to undergo open-heart surgery for the second time. To remember him at sixty-four—his age when they first cut into his chest—was to recall his endurance, strength, and kindness. He had the bulky, knotted forearms of a carpenter; he sported a silver goatee, and he wore wide-framed bifocals that doubled as safety glasses when he patrolled the construction sites he was paid to supervise. When he went in for that first open-heart surgery, everyone knew he would recover. Some joked that anesthesia would be unnecessary. Those who worked under him came to visiting hours at the hospital, and they pictured Charlie waking up while the doctor was sewing his chest back together. Their boss would reach out, wrap his hand around the bicep of the young doctor, and say, "That last stitch was a tad off-line. Would you like this old man to show you how it's done?"

No one seemed surprised when he became, after surgery, both stronger and wiser; not only had he faced down death, but he had emerged with more artery space and a brand new heart valve—he wasn't dead, he was a significantly more efficient breather. He liked to show off the evidence. With the slightest provocation, he would unbutton or pull up his shirt, revealing for anyone not too squeamish the telltale scar that ran like a train track down the middle of his rib cage. He was back on the job in less than two weeks. He moved slowly, but he was there.

He didn't get to stay there long, however. He was forced to retire soon after he turned sixty-five. He tried to establish himself as a fix-it man for hire, a local, reliable, friendly doer of odd jobs. He ordered several hundred business cards and he painted his name, phone number, and FIX-IT-UP MAN on the doors of his pick-up truck, but work was hard to come by. He sat in the house, unemployed, hoping for the phone to ring, wondering what to do with so much free time. Then, suddenly, something changed. The phone started to ring more often, but no one was calling about work. They were calling to share terrible news. The people he'd known for years were dying.

Milly and Charlie found themselves spending much of their sixties and seventies moving from bedside to bedside, trying to cheer their friends and families through long and short final moments. They would hold hands and look each other in the eyes and they would think and not say, If the Gurbargs, the Maisels, the Marins, the Goodmans, and the Maurers can die, how are we to believe that we can keep going much longer?

And yet the doctors spoke to Charlie as if he were the same man at seventy-four that he'd been at sixty-four. They talked in confident voices of increased blood flow and stronger lungs, and they quoted statistics about a new kind of artificial valve made from the heart of a pig. Only a few people heard Charlie's laughter anymore, and they did not hear it often, but Milly remembered him chuckling as he wondered aloud what his father would have thought of such an implant. "What's wrong with the heart of a cow?" he asked the doctors. "Pig valves, you know, they're *tref*. Aren't there valves on the hearts of kosher animals?"

Most of the time, though, Charlie spoke like someone on his way out. At temple, the day before he went to the hospital, Milly overheard him saying such things as "I've had seventy-five good years" or "I've had the pleasure of celebrating my fiftieth wedding anniversary." "The time has come for me to be a little flat on my back," he said. "What can you expect? I can't complain. I haven't had a life you can complain about."

MILLY WAS NOT WAITING long in "the Sunroom" before she saw a friend. Harold Packel, the rabbi of Philadelphia's Congregation Beth Am, was a tall, wide, well-fed man. His suit was simple and black, but his *kepah* was embroidered with gold, blue, silver, and red. Five days a week, he drove to several hospitals, rode the elevator to the top floor of each one, and slowly worked his way down to the lobby, visiting his ailing congregants. He pulled up a chair and sat down beside Milly. "You know, you're not alone here," he said. "Already I've seen Joe Rothstein in intensive care, and Alfred Mutz is getting ready for eye surgery. Marc Hornig's right arm is being put in a cast. Also I ran into Ellen Frank."

"What's Ellen here for?" Milly asked. "Is she visiting, too?"

"No, they were taking her into X-ray, but I don't think she'll be staying overnight."

"Is there anyone else?"

Rabbi Packel took a small blue memo pad out of his shirt pocket, flicked some pages, and said, "Well, I have written down that I should look for Milt Singer around the delivery room because his granddaughter's due for twins. And then there's Meyer Levin, you know, he's a regular volunteer here. You'll see him come strolling by in his uniform." He closed the pad, placed it back in his pocket, and then he leaned forward in his seat. "When I stopped by Charlie's room," he said, "the nurse wouldn't let me in. Tell me, Milly, how is he?"

"Surgery first thing in the morning," she said. "And the doctor told us it might take a long time because he's not exactly sure what he'll find—six, maybe eight, hours. He says there will be scar tissue from the first surgery and that makes it especially difficult."

The rabbi stood up, Milly stood up with him, and they hugged. "I should continue on my rounds before it gets too late," he said. "Is there anything I can do for you while I'm out and about?"

"With all these people in the hospital," Milly said, "we should play poker. Could you tell people where I am when you see them? Ask them to come by and play a few hands with me before they leave. Just penny ante."

"Okay. I'll spread the word," the rabbi said, stepping back toward the bustling crowd of patients and staff and passersby.

MILLY, HUNGRY AND TIRED, sat by herself in "the Sunroom." She wanted to go home and she wanted to take Charlie with her. But she stayed put, turning to face the windows so she could watch the sky grow darker outside. She saw a bus drive into the parking lot and it made her think of her friends and acquaintances who occasionally traveled to Atlantic City casinos. She knew plenty of people who made those trips in search of a jackpot, a tumble of coins, a stack of chips, enough money to remove all worries from their retirement. But she also knew most of her friends went to the glitzy buildings for a different reason. They went to Atlantic City because at the slot machines, or the blackjack table, or at craps or roulette, they could experience the workings of chance and suffer only financial loss. They could step into a world of possibility, play for normal stakes, and it was not impossible to win. Even more, regardless of whether

they won or lost, at the end of the day, everyone ate dinner together, and the bus waited to take them all home.

Before she drifted into a nap, Milly was thinking that the
hospital was a casino of health, well lit around the clock, and
she was wondering how many times you could walk out feeling
better or even feeling the same. How many times could you put
your open heart on the table and get it back?

II.

Because Meyer Levin wisely filched ten boxes of toothpicks
from cafeteria supply, he was given the dual honor of calling
and dealing the first game. He began by explaining how the
toothpicks would serve as poker chips — "a penny a stick" was
the rule — and, acting as the bank, he gave each player a box in
exchange for five dollars. Then he looked around the table and
said, "Ladies and gentlemen, we shall open the evening with a
game of Meshugennah Hurdy-Gurdy." Including Milly, there
were seven people ready to ante up. Marc and Ellen had made
it — Marc with his forearm in a cast and a blue sling, Ellen with
complaints about the personally degrading nature of X-ray pro-
cedure. Milton came over from delivery, and he sat on the edge
of his seat, waiting to be paged so he could rush off to hear the
first cries of his great-grandchildren. Two of Charlie's Thursday
night bowling-league teammates, Linda Wells and her sister,
Nancy, also showed up. Rob Decker, Nancy's husband, was in
overnight after minor foot surgery, so they had come to visit
him, but they also wanted to find out how long it would take
Charlie to get back on the lanes.

Meyer was bald and pale skinned, with large jowls and a fleshy neck, and he wore thick-lensed glasses that pushed right up against his eyelashes. Those black-framed glasses made him look like an insect, but he had a smooth, gentle voice. "Yes," he said, "it shall be Meshugennah Hurdy-Gurdy. I believe there are several novices at the table, so let me briefly explain the game. This is seven-card poker, dealt two down, four up, one down. When a queen hits the table, you know that the next up card will be wild. If more than one queen comes up, the wild card follows the final queen. Queens in the hole are also wild. And here's the crucial element: if at any time I turn up the queen of spades, the game is dead, everyone antes again, and I reshuffle and redeal."

Milly instinctively disliked the idea of a game that went back and forth between being alive and being dead. To relax, she tried to focus on the lilt of Meyer's voice and the movement of the cards. When Meyer dealt an up card, he would hold it right in front of his glasses, then call it out. A two was a "deuce," a three was a "trey," and he pronounced "nine" as if it had two long syllables: "Nigh-in," he would say. He couldn't see the cards on the table well, but he had a strong memory, and he would offer assessments of the hands along the way, saying such things as "The deuce is no use," "He'll make space for an ace," "What's she trying with the nigh-in?"

Again and again, Meyer turned up the queen of spades; he would toss it out onto the middle of the table and say, "Ladies and gentlemen, this game is dead, and that's the beauty of Meshugennah Hurdy-Gurdy." Five, ten, fifteen times in a row, and the pile of toothpicks that was the pot grew larger and larger. Milly didn't know what the odds were of such a long game, but she had played her share of Meshugennah Hurdy-Gurdy over the years and she'd never before seen the queen of spades so many times in a row.

The rest of the players seemed both excited and puzzled. Milly thought they were making small jokes to avoid thinking about the meaning of their odd circumstance. They talked about the winning straight flushes, the winning five-of-a-kinds they could have had. Milly felt disbelief and shock. The death-dealing card kept coming and she could hardly bear it. The game continued, she grew more and more tired, and she considered closing her eyes, but instead she tried to distance herself in silence, only rarely glancing at her hand. She settled into a rhythm: tossing in toothpicks, listening to Meyer's voice, and again she drifted off.

BEFORE SHE FELL completely asleep, she remembered the way the surgeon, Dr. Irving Kravkow, had explained what would happen. There'd been an early-morning meeting in his hospital office and he'd told them that the surgery would take a long time. Then he offered his brief, step-by-step plan: "We'll open him up, stop the heart, put him on a heart and lung machine, and get down to work."

Milly didn't want to quarrel with the plan, but she did have a question. "How is it that you stop the heart?" she asked.

"It's surprisingly easy. To stop a heart, all you do is touch it. You touch it and it stops."

"You just touch it and it stops?"

"Essentially."

Charlie, who had been quietly listening in the chair beside her, asked, "Well, how do you start it going again?"

"A shock, a small electric shock. It's the most unpredictable part of the operation because there's never any guarantee the heart will start back up."

Whenever Milly tried to sleep after that, she had nightmares about her own heart stopping. She turned to the strangers gathered around her and said, "I think my heart's stopped. I could use some help getting it started again." "How can you speak if your heart has stopped?" they wanted to know. Sometimes a young nurse would appear, but she had very little comfort or advice to offer. Though she was sympathetic, she didn't think anything needed to be done and she wanted Milly to calm down. "Oh, your heart has stopped," the nurse would say, as if she were talking to a flustered child. "That's no good. Now, now. Sit here for a minute. Take it easy." The only people who seemed to understand were Charlie and her friends. When they approached her, she would say, "I'm so glad you're here. I need some help. You see, my heart stopped." They would put a hand on her back or give her a hug. "I know how it is," they'd each say. "Mine stopped, too."

Not long ago, Milly had seen a car accident where a bloodied body on a stretcher was lifted into an ambulance, and that was something else that haunted her. Charlie was driving and they were on their way home from an evening movie when they came upon the flares and flashing red lights. "Don't slow down," Milly said as they approached the scene of the crash. "Just drive right past. I don't want to see a thing." But she saw and she felt sure the person on the stretcher was dead.

There was also the time she saw Ben Lasky suffer a stroke. She and Charlie had gone out bowling with Ben and his wife, Helen. Helen walked off to the bathroom and it was Charlie's turn to bowl, so Milly sat with Ben at the scorer's table, watching and chatting. They were trying to figure out where they should go for dinner when Bob grew quiet, turned in his chair, and stared off toward the front door. Then he said, "Butterfly, butterfly, butterfly," and he began to scratch nervously at his chest. Milly rushed to a phone; the ambulance came quickly and Ben did not die. He developed a stutter.

Only once had Milly seen someone die. When she was still a child, seven years old, her mother took her to visit her great-aunt, Annie, in a downtown hospital, and there she was in a wheelchair by a window, gazing out, slouched down, her big-knuckled, arthritic hands folded in her lap, and Milly looked at those hands, wondering who this woman was, wondering why one of those hands was moving toward her, so she stepped back, not wanting to be touched by such pale, bony fingers, and she turned her head, because she didn't even want to see the fingers, and instead she saw an old man roll out of his bed and thump to the hard floor and stay absolutely still as people ran over and touched him and prodded him and lifted him up and covered him with a white sheet. She didn't turn back to her great-aunt Annie; she stared at the shape of the old man and tried to see where his life had gone because she didn't think it could have left the room so quickly.

CALLS CAME IN for the spadey lady and Milly pictured her out at the edge of her consciousness, shovel in hand, digging a large, wide, circular grave at the center of a green field that was dotted with tombstones. She wanted toothpicks for her work. They could stop the earth from caving in. Toss the spadey lady the toothpicks.

Then someone had a hand on her shoulder and was gently shaking her awake. Her eyes shot open, her body tensed, and she said, "What? What? What is it?" The uniformed man who stood before her with his cart full of janitor's equipment was apologetic. "I'm sorry, ma'am," he whispered. "I saw you here and I thought you were sleeping, but I couldn't tell if you were breathing. I'm sorry. It's very early. You go on back to sleep now." Before she could respond, his back was turned and he was walking away.

Meyer Levin was sound asleep in the next chair. The rest of her friends were gone. The cards and toothpicks were on the white table. Milly watched the janitor walk into the next building and then, except for herself, Meyer, and a few slow-moving, sleepy-eyed young doctors, the hallway of glass was empty. She stretched out her arms and rubbed the back of her neck with her right hand. It was almost three thirty in the morning. She thought she might be able to fall back asleep and she hoped she would stop thinking when she did. She closed her eyes, rested her open hands on her chest for a moment, and said aloud, to no one but herself, "I am still breathing. My heart beats and beats."

III.

When Charlie got home, six days after the surgery, he had a terrible case of the hiccups. Dr. Kravkow had kept him open on the table for close to nine hours. He installed the new valve, performed a quadruple bypass, and since he didn't feel comfortable with the way the scar tissue from the earlier operation had come to hold the heart, he cut the heart free and repositioned it. Then they stitched Charlie up. But over the course of the next two days, they had to go back in twice more to clean up internal bleeding. After all this, Milly thought, after once again dodging death, after slowly struggling back to her, he was being driven crazy by hiccups. When she asked the doctor for reasons, he spoke of cilia on the diaphragm that had been disturbed during surgery. It would take them several additional days to heal. But she wanted a more expansive explanation. She wanted to know how something so absurd could happen. Hiccups and open heart. She wanted to know if there was anyone at all who could see fairness and sense in such an arrangement.

The strangeness of the card game seemed to have set the tone for the recovery. When Meyer woke her up that morning in the hallway, he'd told her about how the game had never really ended. After Milly dropped off—and no one, he said, could bear to wake her up—they kept playing, hoping to finish the one game and see who would win the huge pile of toothpicks. The bets grew larger until, eventually, everyone had pushed all five hundred of their toothpicks into the center of the table. Even then, the game was killed by the card. Everyone simply reclaimed their five dollars. Rabbi Packel stopped by after the surgery and told Milly the game sounded like a theme for a sermon: people kept calling the game dead, and yet it never ended. It was possible to wager everything and lose nothing. The game, in his eyes, could be used to illustrate the power of tradition: tradition always seemed endangered, yet it continued, preserving the shape of time, binding people together. Yes, Milly silently allowed, one could see it that way, but she found herself thinking that Meyer's Meshugennah

Hurdy-Gurdy showed how the sign of death was everywhere, how it couldn't be concealed, how it couldn't be avoided; you could shuffle and shuffle, deal and deal, but the sign of death would keep coming. You could call it whatever you liked. You could call it tradition, but that didn't change what it was.

Although Charlie was home, he couldn't relax and he couldn't sleep. He had medication that was supposed to make him drowsy, but that was all it did. He nodded off for fifteen or twenty minutes, then he stood up and shuffled around their small two-story house. Milly followed him from room to room, watching how his body twitched. Each hiccup raised him up, tilting him forward; he lifted his shoulders every time, as if he were trying somehow to shrug off the unending reflex. These were not the sort of hiccups that a sudden scare could chase away. A look of fear already filled Charlie's eyes, a look that asked, When will it stop? She spoke quietly to him, telling him he would be all right, trying to give comfort, asking him to be still, and she thought of death's many masks, its infinite appearances, how it could show itself on the highway, in a bowling alley, in hospitals, as another car, a flash of light, a tug at the throat.

Charlie had other problems. His stomach was upset, the stitches hurt, his entire body felt weak, and he described thick waves of nausea and dizziness that he could see coming; they rose out of the walls, he said, and they towered above his head, curling over just beneath the ceiling, silent and majestic until they crashed down on top of him. But these waves came only every now and then, while the hiccups were continuous, one each minute, sometimes more. Time passed. Hours. He ate nothing for lunch. For dinner he worked down a few bites of a potato knish. It was an effort to drink a glass of water.

"This is torture," he told Milly, and she could see how it was; like a constant reminder of captivity, the hiccups proved his powerlessness and he would have done anything for them to stop. The sun began to set and it had been a full week since he had entered the hospital. He said, "I should have refused the surgery. This isn't right. I shouldn't be here like this."

He wore baggy light blue boxers and a white tank-top undershirt around the house. By late in the evening the combination of his medication, his frustration, his almost-empty stomach, and his lack of sleep made him slightly delusional. Milly was also tired. To herself she said, I am not well rested by any means. She wanted him to get into bed and lie still so she could lie beside him, hold onto him, calm him down, give him warmth, carry him to sleep with her. But he kept getting up. And when he spoke, he didn't make sense. She worried he might have a stroke. She considered returning to the hospital in the morning.

He wandered down from the bedroom to the kitchen where he found the newspaper, and he ripped it up in long slow tears, dropping the shredded paper onto the floor, and he was saying, "It's not today's, not today's," even though it was. He turned on the TV; he turned on the stereo; he opened the microwave oven; he opened the windows. Milly thought he was getting reacquainted with the house. Then he went back upstairs, into the bedroom, into their walk-in clothes closet, and he said, as if he had come to the end of a long, difficult search, "Here they are. They're right here. This is where they are."

"What?" Milly asked. "What is here?"

"These," he said. "These are what's doing it to me." He stepped into the closet and began tossing out ties and belts, throwing them onto the dark brown hardwood floor. "These are what's doing it to me," he repeated. "These are what's doing it to me." His movement was not frantic, but rhythmic, systematic. Over the years, he had accumulated ties wide and narrow, ties of all colors, neckties, bow ties, bolo ties. He threw them over his head, using both hands, right, left, right, left, without looking back. Milly leaned against the bed, out of range, and watched. There were thin dress belts, shiny black and brown, and there were wider belts, large-buckled, banging loudly against the floor. They whipped back through the air, lines of motion moving out from the closet, and then they slid across the bedroom floor, coiling and uncoiling like snakes.

She saw the muscles of his arms and shoulders and legs flicker beneath his skin and there was something comforting in that. She remembered that when the two of them visited friends and relatives in hospitals all across the tristate area, they'd walk into rooms hand in hand, trying to exude happiness and motivation; their fingers tightened as they tried to hold themselves, their family, and their friends together. They smiled, joked, gossiped, thinking all the while that sickness was something everyone had to get through, even those who weren't sick. Charlie could not sit still in those sterile, drab rooms. She would take a seat by the bed, but he would pace, offering to open a window, to adjust the blinds. He'd arrange the flowers as he spoke. He picked up scraps of paper, threw them toward the trash can, and if he missed, he picked them up and shot again. She knew he missed on purpose.

When all the ties and belts of his life were on the floor, Milly stepped into the closet and stood beside him. He was sweating. A hiccup moved up his back; it shrugged his shoulders. She took his hand and she could feel that he would follow her. She led him to the bathroom, gave him his pills, took him to bed and had him lie down. "Be still," she said, "I'll be back in a minute," but his eyes were already closed. She hoped he would sleep at least until sunrise. It was already after midnight. As bad as he looked, as lost, as down, she knew there was a chance that if he would sleep, he could wake up refreshed, free of the hiccups, beginning to feel better.

MILLY WATCHED HER husband sleep. Now, when she could relax for a little while, she felt wide awake. The very last thing she wanted was time to herself. All week long her fear of being alone had increased. She'd spent one night in the glass hallway, but every other evening during Charlie's stay in the hospital, she'd refused the offers of friends and driven herself home after the final visiting hour. When she walked by herself into the house, the loneliness was overwhelming. The steps to the second floor seemed unusually steep and she leaned on the banister, pulling herself up, one step at a time. Then she would check the alarm clock—she needed to wake up at six to be at the hospital by seven—and she would stretch out on the bed where she waited and waited for sleep. After a few minutes, her eyes adjusted to the dark and she could see the emptiness of her room, but she found herself thinking about the bed beneath her. The frame was polished teak, like the bed of her parents. It was an old gift from her mother, a wedding present, handmade by some immigrant friends.

During one of those nights alone, almost dreaming, Milly remembered a time when she was seventeen. Her mother was forty-eight then and her father had been dead for five years. At seventeen, she thought a lot about boys. She had only recently experienced her first substantial kiss and she looked forward to more, but she didn't think her mother would understand her excitement. Her mother was aging, alone, with a body that was sinking in obedience to gravity and too little movement. But then it was late one night, after a date, after a few more kisses had left her longing, confused, bewildered. Milly walked softly by the master bedroom and saw her mother there, wearing only a nightgown, stretched out above the covers, facedown, one hand reaching for each side of the wide mattress, as if she were trying to embrace it. She must have heard Milly's footsteps because she turned toward the door. Her face was red with tears and crying. "I miss him," she said to her daughter, "I really miss him," and Milly knew then that longing filled the night air, that the need for a touch, a kiss, a close body would not disappear with age.

This memory had drawn her out of bed and she had searched the house that night for the three old penmanship notebooks in which her mother had kept her diary. They had plain brown and black covers, wide-lined white pages. She found them in the den, stacked them on her night table, and read them when she couldn't sleep. The first entry was from 1940 and it consisted of the Pledge of Allegiance, before there was anything about God in it, and a list of seemingly random words: "Sympathy weather delicious stomach perhaps crowd knife knock trade charge learning service original special urge whole crisis delay fatal exempt immediately." In the diary she practiced her English; she tried to improve her vocabulary and her spelling as she recorded parts of her life. She wrote about trips to New York City or to the Jersey shore. She wrote about her permanent wave, about the city during a blackout, about her wartime ladies' club. She wrote that she wanted to "tell about each day like Mrs. Roosevelt." Late at night, alone, Milly folded down the corners of certain pages.

She didn't want any more time to herself, but there was something peaceful about this moment long after midnight in the bedroom. Charlie was back home, breathing in the easy rhythm of sleep as she watched over him. She quietly cleaned up the closet, hanging up the ties and belts, the smell of his sweat all around her. She put on her nightgown, brushed her teeth, washed her face, took the pills she had to take. When she stretched out on the bed beside her husband, she listened to his steady breathing and opened one of her mother's notebooks to a passage she had read many times:

December 27, 1941: My daughter Milly married on the day after Christmas half-past eleven. I got up rather early. I could not sleep. During the night I had lots of dreams. I was afraid to go to the wedding for fear I might break down. It was ten o'clock when Milly came. Good morning mother how do you feel I am all right. She looked at me and I looked at her without saying a word to each other. I went upstairs and had a good cry.

Eleven o'clock all of us were dressed for the wedding. Every one of my children looked nice to me. I was proud of them. At the ceremony I closed my eyes and made believe that my husband was near me. He was there—I meant to say his spirit was with every one of us. My new son-in-law looked sweet, one of his cousins gave a luncheon for us. The luncheon was beautiful. Then we went to the reception in another cousin's home. When I came into the house everything looked so beautiful. I didn't think it could be real. I thought maybe I am dreaming. People started to come and every time people came in my thoughts were about my husband. Everybody looked happy. Who knows what goes on in your heart. Didn't I look happy and everybody told me that I looked nice. I tried very hard to keep up a lot of times. I wanted to have a good cry. But I smiled. People don't like to see you cry. It was a hard day for me. My husband used to laugh and say, You have such big troubles. My heart aches for you.

Milly read her mother's shaky, penciled handwriting, and suddenly she was sure Charlie would get better. The hiccups would go away. He had stronger arteries, a shiny new valve, and years to live. But the loneliness that would come was already there; it had sunk in, deep, in anticipation, and it would dwell beside them, even during their happiest moments.

She got out of bed and walked to one of the bedroom windows that looked out over the neighborhood. She put her face up to the glass. It was cool to the touch and it fogged with her breath. She could see houses in the quiet darkness, a blinking yellow traffic light, parked cars along the street, and up at the corner, a redbrick doctor's office.

She felt lonely, but she also felt that she and Charlie were not the only ones in the house. Her mother was there, and her father, and Charlie's parents, too. And the spirits of her friends stood by her, keeping her company, letting her know she wasn't the first to go through this, reminding her how lucky she was to have her husband, still there, on her bed, recovering. He'd placed his open heart on the table one more time and, somehow, again, he'd gotten it back.

Charlie must have heard her sigh and thought she was crying. He woke for a moment and looked over at her. "What is it?" he asked.

"Nothing," she said. Then she climbed back into bed and moved close to him. He felt warm, calm. "Go back to sleep," she said. "I'm here. I'm right here next to you. I'm holding your hand."

No Rest for the Middleman

My mother tells me stories at bedtime. I tell myself stories after she leaves me in the dark.

My father is Solomon Wolinsky, and he is the hero. He saves my mother, Esther Wolinsky. First he has to save himself. We live in Philadelphia in 1923, but when my father was a little boy like me, he lived outside of Odessa.

"Could he walk to the Black Sea?" I ask.

My mother sits on the edge of the bed, next to me and my pillow. "Yes," she answers. "But there was no beach."

"Did he keep his knives sharp?"

"Yes, Abraham. He had to."

In the Old World, he had an old name. He was Shlomo Woliyniec. He was going to have an important job. Kosher slaughterer. He would kill animals cleanly so everyone could eat. There were rules to follow and he had to learn them all. He had to practice. Rabbis damaged his knives to see if he could make the blades perfect again. He could. When he passed their tests, the rabbis gave him official letters. Then his parents told him to take a boat to America.

"They told him to run away?" I ask.

"It was dangerous to stay," my mother says. "He carried his knives and his letters in his coat." She tucks my blankets tight around me. There is no gray in her black hair. Many people tell her she looks too young to be my mother.

"You ran away from Kishniev," I say.

"You know I did," she says. "I had my three older sisters. I watched them marry and grow pregnant. One after another, they lost their babies — Rachel before giving birth; Leah while giving birth; Miriam a few weeks after giving birth. I was fifteen. My mother told me to go to the New World and have her healthy grandson. I listened to my mother."

"I am her healthy grandson."

"You are, but only because your father caught me. I was walking on Market Street —"

"You were hungry."

"I hadn't eaten in almost three days and I started to fall forward. Everyone was rushing by. I didn't have the strength to put my hands out in front of me. Instead, I used them to cover my face. Then I felt other hands under my shoulders, keeping me from hitting the ground."

"I know what he said."

"You do?"

"He said, 'I am Solomon Wolinsky. I will feed you.'"

"That's right, Abraham," she says, kissing my forehead and standing up. "That's just what he said. Now, what do I say?"

"You say it's late."

"I say close your eyes. I say listen to your mother and go to sleep."

I DO NOT FALL asleep right away, but I do listen to my mother. Our apartment is small and I can hear her talk with my father. I know they are sitting together in the kitchen, sharing a glass of red wine. My mother has the glass by herself when my father works late. On those nights, I fall asleep fast because there are no voices. Tonight they are discussing tomorrow—a Sunday, one week after Rosh Hashanah. Since I'm seven and since I asked and asked, I will follow my father to synagogue in the morning. I have been before but never for the whole day and never just with my father.

"He was tired," my mother says.

"I'm tired, too," my father says. "Diamond and Hess won't let up."

"Did you talk to them?"

"I avoided them. Same as yesterday. I stayed in the sanctuary and then I walked home the long way."

"Is there anybody else?"

"Just a few, but only Diamond and Hess matter."

"Maybe Abraham shouldn't go tomorrow," my mother says.

I hear my father's footsteps. He's pacing. His hands are probably behind his back, his head tilted down toward the floor. "I told him I'd take him," he says.

"Just let him sleep. He's tired."

"It will be all right."

A chair is pushed back. Water runs in the sink, drowning out their talk. More footsteps. They're going to their bedroom and they'll close the door and after that their voices will be murmurs. The last words are my mother's, from farther away. I try to hear them all. "He doesn't know," she says. Their door clicks shut.

What don't I know? What do I know? I know about the High Holidays. A little. Sometimes people don't behave. They do things that are wrong. God keeps track. Every year, during the ten days between Rosh Hashanah and Yom Kippur, he sits high above with three giant books open on his desk: the Book of Life, the Book of Death, and the Book of Those-Who-Are-in-the-Middle. God writes the names of the people who behaved all year in the Book of Life and they live for another twelve months. He writes the names of the people who misbehaved in the Book of Death, and they die, maybe not right then, but soon. "Most of us," my father told me, "are in the middle. We have these ten days to repent. God will listen and inscribe us in the Book of Life."

I know my father sold his knives years before I was born. He showed the rabbis' letters to people all over the city, but no one would hire him. They didn't need him. I've seen those knives only in my dreams. Hidden in his black overcoat. Some are longer than others. He used them to kill, but the blades were so sharp that the cows and chickens did not suffer. That's what my mother says. My father told people he needed a job to make money because he had no money. He showed them his open hands, turned up in front of him. Empty. He was eighteen. They could see how his fingers bent strangely from holding his knives for hour after hour. If they shook hands with him, they could feel how his fingers pressed into their palms at odd angles. Like a fortune-teller.

I know about one morning, a long time ago, when my father stopped by a tiny slaughterhouse he hadn't seen before. The owner almost hired him. They talked about money and time. Then a chicken darted out from a cage. It had only one wing. One huge wing. It zipped past the smocked workers. My father says it was a blur of white that ran toward the street. "Grab that chicken!" the owner shouted, but my father stood still and let the unclean bird go free. Who knew how far a one-winged chicken could run? Would someone else catch it? Would another young slaughterer chase it? My father didn't care. "I suppose I've done enough killing," he said. He went right to a pawn shop to sell his knives. "There must be other ways to make a living," he told himself. He decided to be someone different.

I ask, "Why? Why did you let the chicken go?"

"You want to know," my father says, "why I let the chicken cross the road?"

"No, no," I say. "No jokes. Why did you sell your knives? Why did you stop killing?"

Then he tells me about the angel born with only one wing. He kept trying to fly. He jumped up with all his might. He leapt off of mountain tops. He wanted his wing to lift him high into the air. But he fell and he fell and he fell. He broke his legs. He broke his arms. Some people who found him wondered how an angel could look so terrible. Kind people nursed him back to health, and he wandered off to try again. He fell, he hurt himself, he got better.

"But tell me why you sold the knives," I say to my father. "I want to know. I want to know more."

"Imagine that poor angel," my father says. "Wandering, falling, hurt, healing. Wandering, falling, hurt again."

I AM AWAKE before my parents. I make my bed and get out my dress clothes. When I hear my father in the bathroom, I go to keep him company while he shaves. The mirror fogs from the steam. It squeaks when my father wipes it clean. The closed toilet is my chair.

"So," he says, "you're up."

"I dreamt about the chicken again," I say. I like the way his face comes out from underneath the shaving cream. I watch and hope he won't cut himself. But if he does, I'm ready to hand him a piece of toilet paper.

"Is it a scary dream?" he asks.

"I don't think so."

"You know," he says, "I had a scary dream."

"Really?" Sometimes he worries about the wrinkles on his forehead and the sparkles of silver in his hair. He says he's almost closer to forty than to thirty. But I've never heard him talk about a bad dream.

He turns to look at me for a moment. I'm looking right at him and he smiles. There are dots of foam near his ears and on his neck. "No," he says. "I can't even remember the dream. I was really thinking that I should have caught that chicken."

"Caught it?"

"I could have brought it home. It could have been our pet and you could have taken it for walks. That would have been something to see."

"Would it have laid eggs for us?"

"Maybe."

I imagine making a nest in my bedroom. I'd like to hear clucking in the mornings. "Do you think the baby chickens would have just one wing?" I ask.

My father rinses off the razor, then his face. "I don't know," he says, "but I do know it's time for you to wash up and get dressed." I throw him a small towel and he catches it. "Your mother is probably waiting for you," he says.

She is in my room. "You don't have to go if you don't want to," she says. "We could spend the day together."

"I want to go," I say. I put on the white shirt and button it up to the top. Everything else is brown—the woolly pants, vest, and jacket. The tie and shoes and socks. My mother's fingers fuss with them all. "Breathe in," she says, tightening the vest.

She follows us to the front door. On her tiptoes, she reaches up to kiss my father. She squats down to get me. "Stand up straight, Abraham," she says. "Obey your father."

WE'RE OUT OF the house before sunrise, walking together in the dark, up Ellsworth Street to Sixty-third, then down toward Market Street and Temple Beth Israel.

"Father," I say, and my voice seems too loud for the quiet streets.

"Shh," he says. "Think about earning forgiveness."

We walk in silence for a few minutes. Almost everyone must be asleep. "Why do we need to be so early?" I whisper.

"You want to know about the early bird?"

"No, no."

"All right," he says. "I'll tell you why."

"I'll listen," I say.

"What's my job?" he asks.

"You get things for people."

"Yes. People pay me and I get them the things they want. But sometimes they pay me and I can't get them what they want right away. They might want their money back. But I don't keep their money. It does me no good to hold it in my hands. I can't just give it back because I use it to buy other things. Then people can get angry."

My father never talks so much about his work. I want him to keep going. He's looking around while we walk. I try to make sure my questions are good questions. "Do you ask them to wait?"

"I ask them, but they usually don't want to wait. And it can take a long time. So I need to pray for forgiveness. It's important to be generous during the High Holidays. Patient, too. It's not a time for meanness. You know we're not the most Jewish family, but everyone wants to be in the Book of Life."

"How angry do people get?" I ask.

"That's a good question, Abraham. It depends. There seems to be more anger lately."

At the corner of Sixty-third and Market, the El runs above our heads. We stand still, listening to the thundering rattle, the high whistle of the brakes. I see two men at work in a bakery, carrying trays of dough. An old man pushes a cart full of shiny apples. Some people step off the train, others step on. I look for anger in their faces.

WE'RE THE FIRST to arrive at Temple Beth Israel and we go right to our seats in the cold sanctuary. The walls must be thin or full of holes. The wooden chairs are not comfortable. I think our religion is nicer at home because we don't have to dress up. People don't come and go there. In our kitchen, my mother lights the candles on the Sabbath. My father says the blessing for the wine and I say the blessing for the bread. But I do like watching what happens on the bimah. The rabbi will carry the Torah above his head. The cantor will sing. The rabbi will spread his arms wide to welcome us.

My father says I can take a nap while we wait for services to begin, but I don't want to. I fight to stay awake. I want to remember everything I did wrong. When I was yelled at. When I lied. The handful of nickels I took and hid. The times I pretended to be asleep.

My father's head tilts down and he closes his eyes. He's thinking. When I stand up to go use the men's room, he says, "If anyone bothers you, here's what you tell them. You tell them you are not permitted to make promises for me."

There are people in the lobby. I walk quickly past them. In the bathroom, I have my choice of urinals. Then two men come in behind me. They are older than my father, and bigger. They make the room feel crowded.

"There he is," the first one says.

"The little Wolinsky," says the second one, laughing.

I inch closer to the white porcelain. I'm not completely done, but I stop and zip up. "Good *yontif*," I say, on my way to the sink.

"Yes, yes," the first one says. "A good *yontif* to you, too."

"And to your father," says the man who is no longer laughing.

"Of course," says the first, "if you're going to give him our good wishes, you'll need to know who we are."

They are blocking the door. The first man keeps talking. His voice is almost kind, like a teacher's. "I'm Mr. Phil Diamond and that's Mr. Ronald Hess. We'd like a chance to speak with your father, but we know from experience that will be difficult. So we're speaking to you. We'd like to ask your father to return something of ours. And we know he'll be generous for the next few days, with so much at stake."

"The Book of Life is open to those who seek forgiveness," says Hess. His voice is not kind. It is rough and strong, like a truck engine.

"What do you say, little man?" asks Diamond.

"I can't promise you anything," I answer.

"You just tell him you saw us," Diamond says. "We'd speak with him ourselves if he'd step outside the sanctuary."

"He's busy," I say.

"He can't stay in there all day long again," Hess says.

"I hear he has a special diet for the High Holidays," Diamond says.

"I hear a lot of things," Hess says, stepping closer to me at the sink. I step back and wonder if I'm fast enough to lock myself in one of the stalls. Hess turns on the hot water all the way.

I see anger in his face, especially in his thick, black eyebrows, so heavy that he has to squint. "How long do you think he would stay out there if you didn't come back?" he asks.

I watch the hot water. It rises up in the sink, but it does not overflow.

"Cut it out, Ron," Diamond says.

"Thirty minutes? An hour? Eventually, he'd have to come looking. How long has it been?"

"We wouldn't hurt you," Diamond says. "No one's saying that, so don't worry. We just might make you comfortable somewhere for a while."

"What do you know about your father?" Hess asks.

"I know he's a hero," I say.

"Sure he is. If heroes steal. If heroes are weasels. If heroes don't keep their word."

"That's enough, Ron."

"Let me tell you this, little man. Your father—"

"I said that's enough."

"Your father is in trouble. That's all I wanted to say."

"This is a small boy," Diamond says. "This is two days before Yom Kippur. You decide how far you want to go."

Hess puts his hands up, just above his shoulders, like someone being robbed. "I'm standing here talking," he says. "I'm checking the temple's hot water. I'm not going too far." He drops his hands and picks up a few cloth towels from a pile by the sink.

The bathroom door finally swings open and two more men walk in. Diamond and Hess give them space, watching me closely. Nobody says anything. The new men look away. I wonder if it would be better for me to shout or run. I could do both. Then my father comes in. He sees me and holds out his hand. "Let's go, Abraham," he says.

He's standing between Diamond and Hess. Diamond takes a step back. Hess dips his hand, wrapped in the towels, down into the sink and he splashes my father with the hot water. In his face and all over the front of his suit. My father reaches inside his jacket and I wait for one of the knives to come out. The perfect blade will shine. The men will rush toward the door. But my father pulls out a white handkerchief and dries his face, red like it is after shaving. He folds the handkerchief carefully before putting it back in his pocket. "Let's go, Abraham," he says again. "We're done in here."

"You may be done in here," Hess says, turning off the water. "But you're not done."

"We're leaving," my father says. "See me after Yom Kippur. You know I run my business alone. My son has no part in this."

"That's one way to look at it," Hess says. "But here's how I see it. You take something of ours. We might take something of yours."

The two men who came in before my father stand with their backs to the urinals. They are ready to leave, but they can't get to the sink or the door. "This is not the time," one of them says. "This is not the place. Services are about to start."

"The Book of Life and the Book of Death," Hess says. "The Book of Pain and the Book of Suffering."

"All right," Diamond says. "We've made our point."

"For now," says Hess.

"Let's go, Abraham," my father says.

"I need to wash my hands," I say.

Hess moves toward the door. "Go ahead," he says, and then he turns his back, walking out behind Diamond.

My father's clothes are still wet when we walk across the lobby a few moments later. We enter the sanctuary. People are quiet when we pass by.

I WANT TO understand more. There are prayers I wish I could sing together with my father. There are prayers that seem to go on forever.

The rabbi tells a long story about a place on the other side of the world. I listen as closely as I can. He says that everything in the world has a heart and the world itself has one very large heart and this large heart beats at the top of a high mountain, near a clear spring that flows from a gigantic rock. Every night, after the sun sets, the heart beats more slowly and the world starts to die. Then the clear spring sings to the heart. The heart of the world strains to sing back. Their singing echoes, and shining threads grow out of the songs and reach every living thing, connecting one heart with another. And then there is one just man who is chosen by God. He wanders through the world before sunrise, gathering the shining threads from every heart. He weaves the threads into time. When he has woven a full day of time, he gives it to the heart of the world. Then the heart of the world is revived and begins to beat strongly again.

I look at my father and he knows that I have questions. "It shows how fragile we are," he whispers.

"How precariously we are balanced," says the rabbi. "Without forgiveness, we cannot last."

I stand and sit beside my father. Again and again, I tell God I'm sorry for not being better. I pray that he'll keep us away from death. I imagine visiting the other side of the world, the mountain, the rock, and the spring. Would it be different from the world of the Black Sea, Odessa, and Kishniev? When I grow up, I want to be a surgeon, but I'd like the job of gathering everyone's shining threads. I'd carry each one carefully and people would always be happy to see me. I look at the crowd around us, trying to find Hess and Diamond. I think they're gone. I wonder if they're praying.

We don't leave the sanctuary until long after the end of services. The whole temple is empty when we start to walk home in the dark, through backyards and parking lots, avoiding the streets. As soon as he can, my father unzips in a secluded corner, behind a closed pharmacy.

"No rest for the middleman," he says to me as I piss with him.

I'm done before he is. He goes on for minutes and maybe the sound gives us away. We hear footsteps and a voice behind us. "Good evening, Solomon. We had more to tell you."

My father knows who it is without looking and he does not stop what he's doing. "All right," he says. "My heart is open. I'll have it for you tomorrow, holiday or no holiday."

"I'm glad to hear that," Hess says. "Still, I have to give you this message. Phil asked me not to. But I feel it's necessary. So we reached a compromise. He'll take your son home while you and I have our discussion."

My father has finished at last. He turns to face Hess and Diamond. He stands up straight and I follow his example. I press my feet into the ground. "Is this the way it has to be?" he asks.

"It is," Hess answers.

"All right," my father says, and then he puts a hand on top of my head. He looks down at me and says, "You go with Mr. Diamond, Abraham. He'll take you home and you tell your mother I'll be there soon."

"I can wait," I say.

"I know you can, but I want you to go. I'll meet you there. I'll be fine."

Diamond steps closer to me. "Forget those things we told you in the bathroom," he says. "I'll take you right home. I give you my word."

"Go on," my father says.

I obey him and walk in front of the store, back to the street. I turn around once before we're out of sight. I see Hess and my father standing side by side in the dark, as if they were best friends who wanted to be left alone.

Farther down Sixty-third Street, Diamond says, "You spent the whole day in the temple, little man. Do you want to be a rabbi when you grow up?"

"I want to be a surgeon," I say.

"I see," he says. "Medicine's a good business to be in."

"I'll have a scalpel," I say. "I'll keep it sharp."

"You'll be able to make sure your mother and father stay healthy."

"What will happen to my father?"

"He'll be all right today," Diamond answers. "You know, I have a son, older than you, and I wonder what will happen to him. It's hard for me to be sure. His name is Charlie. I'll tell you this, a son can do a lot to change a man. Maybe your father will surprise me."

"What will your friend do to him?"

"I'm thinking of getting a different job myself," Diamond says, as if he didn't hear my question. "It's a bad business we're in, your father and I. It's no way to raise a family."

"Is he hurting my father?"

"I'm not going to lie to you, little man," he says, putting his hand on my back and giving me a push with his fingers. "There's Ellsworth Street. You can make it home from here. Go on and tell your mother not to worry."

I run the rest of the way.

My mother gives me a hug and we pretend. I think if I cried, she would, too. "Mr. Diamond walked me home," I tell her. "Mr. Hess had a message for Father. I wanted to stay with him, but he told me to go. He said to tell you he'd be home soon."

We have our dinner and we hardly talk at all. I eat more than she does. We want to hear the door open.

"Did you like the services?" she asks.

"Yes," I say. "I asked for forgiveness and I didn't take a nap."

"Are you tired now?"

"Yes."

"Why don't you go get ready for bed," she says. "After your father comes home, I'll tell you a story."

In my room, I take off my dress clothes and put them neatly on my chair. I stretch out in bed and I listen. My mother does the dishes. She paces. I fight to stay awake.

When I hear my father's voice, I sneak out of my room. I stay close to my door and they don't notice me. "That bastard," my father says. "He didn't have to do this." He's sitting by the kitchen table. My mother is standing behind him, washing blood from his face and hair. "Shh," she says. "We'll be all right. Don't wake Abraham." She leans over him and holds him up in the chair with her hand on his shoulder. After the blood is gone, I can see the bruises and the cuts. His face is the wrong shape, the skin puffy, red and purple and dark. One eye is black, swelling shut. I stop staring and run toward him. He turns to me and I'm getting closer and I know he'll never look the same again.

Distance Man

I once thought I would be younger forever. For years my older brother, Adrian, reminded me of my place. When the mood struck him, he struck me.

What would have happened if there had been more of us? A few more brothers? A sister or two? Maybe Adrian and I would have grown up closer.

We lived near Morriston, a decaying paper-mill town sixty miles north of Philadelphia, and everything around us — houses, schools, streets — had just about finished falling apart. We weren't poor, and like most of our neighborhood, we had enough to remain comfortable for a while. The mothers and fathers of our community would be able to keep their jobs, but there would be nothing to hand down to the children. As a result, our generation learned early on that we'd need to find a way to leave. Some got work in Allentown or Philly, some married and moved out-of-state, a few went to college. If Adrian and I had been surrounded by other siblings, we might have united and escaped together.

But it was just the two of us.

Our parents were tired from working extra hours and they left us to take care of ourselves whenever possible. They were too busy to remember the kind of information I wanted.

"What was the first thing Adrian did to me?" I occasionally asked my mother.

"Oh, Alex," she'd say. "All this will pass."

Then she'd quickly go on to tell me again that Adrian and I were brothers, as if I didn't know. "It will mean a lot to you both someday," she insisted.

I thought the first incident might reveal a clear reason for my brother's behavior. But I could discover no logic. Right before he would hit me, I'd sometimes ask, backing away, "What? What did I do?"

When he said anything at all, he'd say, "It's that look on your face."

So I checked various mirrors in our house, one full length, one a large oval, one a pocket-sized square kept by the front door. I never noticed any upsetting, special look passing over my features, even when I stuck my tongue way out or over-puckered my lips like a fish. I could make plenty of funny faces, some a little scarier than others, but none of them cried out for hitting. Just my face. There it was.

It's true, though, that I did stare right at Adrian for long moments, and maybe such silent, steady attention made him want

to hurt me. I watched how he walked—duck footed and plod-
ding, swaying from side to side with his shoulders, trying to
show toughness with each step. His hands hardly moved when
he talked. I looked at his face to see how it changed when he
entered a room, how his brown eyes narrowed when he listened,
how the bump in the middle of his nose always seemed shiny, as
if the skin had been too tightly stretched there.

After all, with only minor differences, my face was his face
three years younger. If I saw how he moved through his life,
then I could figure out what made him successful in the world
and me not.

HITTING WAS JUST one means of attack. There were
also weeks, months, maybe even entire years when he'd call me
names I didn't understand. As soon as I got hold of a definition,
he'd throw a new name at me. I'd be "Xylophage" one day, then
"Dross-Man," then "Pusillani-Mouse."

When I turned twelve, I suddenly needed glasses for my eyes
and tiny tubes for my ears. While I tried to cope with these
changes, Adrian found a name for me to keep. "Martian," he
called me.

"You're an alien," he went on. "You have physical problems because your body's struggling to adjust to the earth's atmosphere."

"You're the Martian," I told him.

"Who's wearing glasses?" he asked. "Who has water in his
ears?"

"You're the Martian," I repeated.

"No. I was born here and I'm thriving. You were hatched on
a distant planet and dumped like trash into outer space."

Eventually, I stopped resisting, even though my first real memory of Adrian suggests he's as responsible as anyone for the main alien features he identified. In this memory, I'm three and he's six. He's lifting me up and I am happy. This is the way older brothers should behave—raise up the younger ones, help them to reach what they can't grasp themselves. There's something he wants me to do. We lean against the kitchen counter and he's holding me up with my back to his chest, his arms wrapped beneath my rib cage. He tells me to pick up the fork and stick it into the holes on the wall by the toaster.

I don't remember feeling the shock, but I do remember the fork's melted, blackened tines. And it's easy for me to imagine that bolt of electricity shooting through my young skull, damaging the tissue of my eyes and ears.

BY THE TIME I turned thirteen, I had read enough books and seen enough TV to realize that outer space aliens possessed a power all their own. There were definite advantages to being an energetic Martian at my understaffed junior high school. In the middle of class, I would start waving my arms like a drowning child, shouting that I could not breathe this earthly air. "I can't see," I sometimes exclaimed. "My world has gone dark!" And when a teacher or a scared student would say, "Alex, calm down. Please calm down, Alex," I would shout louder. "Oh no, now I can't hear! What did you say? I can't even hear a word I'm saying! What did I just say? Can you hear me?"

Teachers told me to visit the nurse, but I'd head outside, back to the old tennis courts, where I would often find fellow cutters. We'd smoke some cigarettes or walk a few blocks to buy snack food. We were not a particularly bad bunch; we just wanted our days to go differently.

When I turned fourteen and began high school, I was actually glad to learn that I would need braces—I'd have a new routine for my new teachers. During the second week of ninth grade, a few days after the orthodontist had glued and twisted a handful of metal into place around my misdirected Martian teeth, I sat for about three minutes in algebra class before I started moaning and finger-pointing. I tried to communicate that my tongue had become stuck in my braces. Did my aging, overworked teacher fully understand or care what I was saying? It's hard to determine. At some point, it must have been easier for everyone just to let me leave.

New to the high school, I didn't know which direction to go once I left class, so I wandered through the hallways.

To this day, I don't know exactly where Danny DeLue came from that morning. Coach of the swim team and assistant director of physical education, DeLue stood maybe two inches above five feet. He was a powerful man, with shoulders so broad that his red-haired head and freckled face appeared strangely small. He resembled a Martian far more than I did. "De-Loser," Adrian and his friends called him, from a distance.

His job seemed to give him immense satisfaction, and he made the gym a safe place, but at the same time he liked pushing us to our limits. During gymnastics, for instance, if you lost your balance, he'd keep you from banging your head against the beam; he'd catch you if you lost your grip on the rings. But first he would let you reach the point where you knew you were falling. Panic charged through your whole body. Fear filled your thoughts. Then he would save you, stand you gently up on your own two uninjured feet. He wouldn't rub it in. "I've got you," I once heard him say. Or "There you go. No problem. Safe and sound." It was just enough to guarantee you'd never look at him the same way again.

When he appeared from nowhere and surprised me in the empty hallway, he spoke as if he had been waiting for me all morning. "Alexander," he said. "Been looking for you. Come with me."

It took a second, but I recovered my presence of mind enough to say, motioning wildly in the general direction of my mouth, "Nung nuck nin naces. Ny need nurse."

"Let me see," DeLue said. He pulled down on my chin with his right hand and if my tongue had really been attached to my braces, it would have ripped in two.

"You're fine," he said. "Come with me."

"Maybe I should get back to class," I suggested.

"You already left class," he said. "Let's go."

"Where?" I wanted to know.

"Swim test."

ALL THROUGH MY TIME in public school, my teachers seemed to be Adrian's accomplices. He'd hit me, call me names, and then I'd go into class, glad to be out of the house, only to hear how smart and bright and witty my brother was and how I was not the same. "Adrian's not my brother," I would sometimes shout. "I'm a Martian and I'm not related to him at all."

So after I swam one length of the pool, it was a surprise and a pleasure to hear DeLue say, "Good, good. You've got a stroke we can use. Not like your brother, Adrian."

"What?" I asked, just to hear it again.

"I said you can swim, not like your brother, who was a fool in the pool."

I liked the way that sentence echoed off the tiled floors and walls. I immediately nodded yes when DeLue said, "Practice here at three thirty, starting today. All right?"

Even after I changed and left the gym, I did not regret my decision. What did I have to do after school anyhow? Rush home and try to dodge Adrian? Hang out with some back-of-the-bus kids behind the school? Sure, I'd swim.

AFTER A FEW PRACTICES, I decided that DeLue's own appearance must have led him to assemble a team full of outcasts and oddballs. There were only a few boys with traditional V-shaped bodies and they had been swimming for years. Most of the recruits came from DeLue's walks through the hallways and parking lots. Some cut class, others wrote cryptic notes to themselves, and one played the tuba. We had long thin legs or pudgy little hands or too-large stomachs, and early in the season, we all had our heads shaved. I looked so strange with my thick plastic glasses and my bald scalp that my parents rushed me out to get contact lenses.

From the first, DeLue saw me as a distance man. Plenty of people could handle the sprints and relays. "What this team needs right now," he said, "is someone who can go on and on." During practice he would set me off in my own lane, telling me to do one five hundred after another. "Efficiency," he'd say, "that's what we're after." And he'd tell me to swim straighter, to focus on hitting my turns. "No wasted motion," he'd say. "Wasted motion slows you down and tires you out."

Every day he'd lead us up to the balcony, where there were six rows of bleachers for spectators, and he'd make us run. We had to hop up the steps two at a time, then run down, then hop up again, up and down, from one end of the balcony to the other. Our bare feet slapped against the tile floor and DeLue clapped his hands to set the pace. He shouted questions and answers while we huffed along. "When are you fastest in the pool? When you dive in at the start. You're slowing down after that. You need to dive out with your legs! When are you second fastest in the pool? Each time you turn. You accelerate toward the wall, you hit your turn, and you need your legs to push you out into the lead!"

During these bleacher drills there would always be one or two moments when I would find myself on the top stair, waiting for the person in front of me to run ahead. I'd look out over the team, everyone moving quickly through the chlorine-filled air. We were a bunch of barefoot, skin-headed, shaved-legs guys, wearing dark blue Speedo suits. We had goggle indentations around our eyes and we followed the orders of a short, bulky man with a shock of red hair. I wondered what someone walking in off the street would think of us.

And if Adrian and my parents were to step in, would they be surprised to see me amid such a group? Once they picked me out, poised so high above them, would they be puzzled or proud, or both?

If anyone did watch, no matter who they were, they'd eventually see us return to the water for freestyle sprints. DeLue would walk from lane to lane, shouting at us. He'd keep telling us how and when to breathe, as if it were something we had never done before.

DeLue didn't require practice twice a day, but he scheduled optional early-morning swims, and he was there at 5:30 a.m., Monday through Friday, ready to help. Nearly everyone came in. DeLue would offer advice, but there was none of the calling out that filled the afternoon sessions. He kept everything quiet. We'd swim ourselves awake, shower, get breakfast together at a nearby market, and head to class.

Once I was in the routine of swimming before and after school, nothing felt more natural. All through the day, I could smell the chlorine that tightened my skin, and the sharp odor only made me look forward more to afternoon practice. I felt the soreness of my muscles as I walked down the hallways or lifted books out of my locker, but I knew I would be lighter and looser in the pool. When my stroke was on, I could soar, smooth along the surface, making the water rush past me.

Meanwhile, Adrian began to disappear from my life. As a high school senior, he had his college future to arrange. I swam and hardly saw him at all. He busied himself with pamphlets, recommendation forms, and application after application.

Even though the team never came close to winning, my parents attended as many meets as they could and they tried to get Adrian to join them. He was always busy and he'd say, "I don't want to see him bald and in a Speedo."

I WASN'T SURE exactly how it would happen, but I kept believing Adrian and I would become close. We'd learn, over time, to laugh at our growing up. "I don't know what I was thinking," Adrian would say to me, one of his arms draped around my shoulders. "I don't know what my problem was." I'd tell him I understood even if I didn't.

Then his graduation came and went, and we grew no closer. He was going to move to Maine, where a small college had awarded him a scholarship. "All this will pass," our mother had said, but her words seemed true in ways she didn't mean.

That summer I lifeguarded at the YMCA to make a little money, but mainly I worked to become stronger and better looking. I swam often, of course. I also ran and lifted and rode my bike. There were days when I'd put together my own personal triathlon and I'd surprise everybody with the number of miles I could go.

I liked covering so much distance. Back roads stretched from Morriston west to Allentown, and you could ascend for miles, then ride along a ridge and gaze out over the paper-making valley. From far away, the industrial seemed scenic. The sense of decay, so obvious from our front door, disappeared, and I saw instead a gentle oasis protected by rolling hills. It didn't look like the kind of town anyone would ever want to leave.

But Adrian didn't hesitate. On the day he was to drive north, I woke up early and took a long bike ride. When I returned, he was almost set to go. He stood beside his rusty, green Jeep and he checked to make sure everything he possessed was carefully packed. He looked light on his feet, as if he were already just visiting.

"Here's Alex," he said. "Now I'm out of here."

My parents hugged Adrian and he patted their backs, look-ing over their shoulders, staring at something out beyond our squat house. When he stopped in front of me, he extended his hand. It was offered and empty, not balled into a fist, and I wondered, How is it that in all of these years I have never hit him? I'd become strong enough and there were certainly times when I could have made him feel directly some of the frustra-tion and anger I'd stored up for so long. I knew then, standing before him, that I'd never hit him because I feared it would separate us further. I'd never hit back because I feared he would leave and here he was, leaving.

If I had been older or different, I might have brushed his hand aside, wrestled him to the ground, and forced him to hold me in his arms. "Be nicer," I could have shouted into his star-tled face. "It wouldn't hurt you to be nicer." Instead, I tried to convince myself that I didn't need him. If he wanted to shake hands, then I could shake hands.

DURING THE YEARS that followed, Adrian appeared in a persistent disaster dream of mine. I'd fall asleep and then we'd be sitting together in a simple wooden rowboat out on the ocean. Adrian had the oars, but only for an instant because the dream carried us into the center of a raging storm, complete with monsoon rain, enormous waves, hurricane winds. The boat vanished and it became impossible to distinguish the dark rough sea from the dark drenched sky. For me, the distance man, it was only water, and I stayed afloat. Lifted to the top of wave after wave, I saw the shore, not too far away. I knew immediately that Adrian wouldn't be able to make it on his own, so I swam toward him.

Once I was close to him, I waited until the last second. I watched my older brother go under, his arms flailing, his wide eyes looking to me for help. Up he bobbed again, his head breaking through the surface of the water, and he breathed in as much air as he could. I heard him gasping. I watched him sink down once more as I floated with ease. I knew I could grab hold of my brother and pull him out of danger. It wouldn't be difficult at all. As he came up again, he reached his open hand out to me, and I reached for him, speaking to him, shouting so he could hear, "I've got you, Adrian! Don't worry!"

I did have him. For a moment, I held on, my arm wrapping around his chest. Then, just before I woke up, I looked and saw the rough water covering his head.

I SWAM AND SWAM through high school, and predictably, it was through swimming that I found my career. "Hey Alexander," DeLue asked me one day, "what are you going to do with yourself after you graduate?"

"I have no idea."

"Have you thought about diving?"

"I'm a distance man, coach. I don't dive."

"Not that kind of diving. I mean diving as in deep-sea diving, as in marine biology."

Community college followed, then a master's program at Penn State, and then a job with the United States Department of Fisheries that sent me to North Carolina. Now, nearly two decades after high school, I tell people what I do, and I can

DISTANCE MAN | 51

watch the wrong impression wash over their faces. Saying I'm a marine biologist is like announcing that I'm an astronaut or, better, an alien, for it's my access to a completely other world that tends to interest everyone. So they can understand what I do and what I don't, I try to dispel their illusions immediately.

"I work for the government," I say, "not for Jacques Cousteau, may he rest in peace."

I perform simple damage assessment and my dives are not complex. Based in Beaufort, I check the population of sea grasses in the shallow, well-traveled waters around the Outer Banks. I monitor the destructive effects of pollution and way-ward ships. I have colleagues who do more glamorous work and their studies of dolphins, sharks, and herons attract considerable attention and funding for our lab. My research, in comparison, is extremely low profile. I putter just offshore in a small motor-ized rowboat. I zip on a wet suit, drop myself overboard, and sink down to the bottom. I stay there counting roots and shoots until my air runs out. It may not sound particularly thrilling, but I love my work: I do good, solid science.

In my own way, I have been successful. As has Adrian. He cruised easily through college, found a sweetheart named Julia, moved on to an MBA, married, and bought a house just outside of Boston. They had a daughter named Anna, and then, two years later, a second child, a son named Turner.

I have no wife, no children, and lately, no hair. Once a Mar-tian, always a Martian, or so it sometimes seems to me. Adrian works with people; I work underwater. He makes a great deal of money; I do not.

Our parents were proud of us both to the end. Whenever

they saw us, they said how pleased they were with our progress. One at a time, they passed away. "Take care of each other," they said as they departed, and we smiled at them before returning to our separate lives.

I continued imagining conversations Adrian and I would have. We'd have so much to say, so many plans to make for a different future. But my nightmare was more accurate: I reached out, he slipped away. I tried to visit, I called to talk, but there was never a good time for me to go to Boston, and more often than not, it was Julia who answered the phone to tell me in her happy voice that Adrian was busy. "I don't understand why the two of you don't get along," she occasionally said.

I AM CERTAIN she is the one who made Turner's visit possible. Maybe the gifts I sent north to Boston helped—a snorkel and mask, flippers, a small aquarium—or maybe he watched certain TV shows, or maybe it was just a natural consequence of his being the younger child. For whatever reason, at age twelve, Turner began to tell people he wanted to be a marine biologist. So one night, out of the blue, Julia called and arranged for him to travel south for a few days between Christmas and the new year.

He arrived late in the evening, ready for sleep, but he was clearly excited when I told him we'd get up early in the morning and take a motorboat out on the water. We had never spent much time together, and I had not seen him at all in four years. I led him to the car, thinking how strange it was to have him walking by my side across the well-lit New Bern airport parking lot. Adrian's son, a bounce to his step, a backpack over his shoulder, a little man looking up into my eyes. "Uncle Alex," he said, and a moment passed before I realized he was speaking to me.

"Nephew Turner," I replied, taking his backpack into my hand.

"Will we go fishing tomorrow on the boat?"

"No. We'll do something better."

"Diving?"

"Better."

AFTER HE FELL ASLEEP on my futon couch, I called in to Boston. Julia answered and I told her Turner had arrived safe and sound.

"Isn't he cute?" she asked.

"He's great," I said. "So grown up. He walks like a little man."

"Adrian says he looks just like you used to look."

I paused. "Does he smile when he says that?"

"Not really," she said.

I AWOKE TOO EARLY and couldn't get back to sleep, so I let my mind fill with questions. They were questions for Turner, and I resisted the temptation to wake him up. What have you heard about me? I wanted to ask. What is it like around your house from day to day? How does your older sister treat you? How do you get along with your father?

As the first light began to shimmer on the water, I walked quietly through the living room and into the kitchen to make coffee. I watched Turner sleeping. I noticed his outsized feet and hands, his blond hair, the fair face of his mother, the broad shoulders of his grandfather, and I imagined him taller than us all, buck-handsome and strong. Still, there on the futon, he looked small to me, and new. Despite what Julia had said on the phone, Turner reminded me most of my brother—a much younger version, on the edge of growing and changing. When I reached out to touch his shoulder, I could feel myself holding my breath. I could almost hear the peaceful, resting rhythm of his heart, and I was telling myself: Don't talk too much. Don't talk too much. Don't scare him away.

BECAUSE ONE OF MY FRIENDS had left town for the holidays, I had been able to make special arrangements for Turner—he'd get a taste of the more glamorous side of marine biology. Twice a week, my friend had to monitor the dolphin population at several specific sites around Cape Lookout. I helped with his project from time to time and I'd agreed to fill in for him while he was away. As we left the apartment, I told Turner we would spend the day counting dolphins. He rushed outside.

Beaufort seemed very quiet, and there was no one else around the dock when we stepped into the lab's twenty-one-foot Parker. The forecast called for calm weather, little wind, and I was happy to see smooth water stretching out before us. Turner was smiling, looking everywhere. If there had been a crow's nest, he would have climbed right up to it, binoculars in hand, to see all he could see.

We started out, and for a while there were only gulls. I liked the anticipation that filled Turner as he kept watch. We closed

in on Cape Lookout and I showed him the lighthouse, a land-
mark that would be in sight throughout the day. Then I showed
him the first spot where we'd be stopping, marked by a buoy,
but also marked by movement in the water. I cut the motor as
we drew up.

The dolphins were right there, swimming around us, arc-
ing out of the water, slipping over one another. They appeared
so playful and powerful, churning through the surf, splashing, diving. Turner darted from side to side, from bow to stern.
"There's another!" he shouted. "That's five! No, nine! Twelve!
Seventeen!"

His voice didn't disturb the dolphins. In fact, I dropped a
microphone into the water, switched on the speaker, and we
could hear them squeaking and chirping to each other. Turner
stood still and listened. "Awesome!" he said, and then he was
off again, moving all over the boat.

It takes practice to learn how to get an accurate count. It's
important, for instance, to pay attention to the direction the
dolphins are traveling. It's also helpful to focus on the shape of
the fins that rise out of the water, since each dolphin's dorsal fin
is distinctive. I was looking forward to teaching Turner more
about my friend's project, but there was no rush. It was a pleasure for me just to watch him for a while. I wanted to remember
the details of his happiness—the sound of his voice, how he
kept standing on his tiptoes, the way he waved his hands above
his head, as if he were sending signals of joy to approaching
ships.

I didn't have a plan when after a few minutes I stepped behind Turner and lifted him up. He wasn't very heavy. I had my

balance, and with my hands on his waist, I held him up high, like a sacrifice. He probably thought I was just helping him to get a better view of the beauty surrounding us. He laughed and pointed out toward the horizon. At first, I was laughing, too, but then I found myself looking down at the deep, cold water, imagining what would happen if I dropped Turner overboard. It would be a terrible thing to do and it was an awful thing to picture. Yet once I started, I could think of nothing else. I could almost see his slow-motion fall, the windmill of his thin arms, surprise and disbelief and incomprehension flickering across his tender face. How could he understand something like this? He couldn't, of course, but his father might. My mind moved to other, more practical questions. Would Turner panic when he hit the water? Would he be able to climb up into the boat on his own? Would I dive in after him? Would I wait until the last second, as I waited in my dream? Would he cry out for me?

Right beside the boat, two dolphins arced into the air, splashed down, and slapped the water with their tails, soaking us with sea spray while I considered all I could destroy and how quickly. Then I began talking, reciting some of what I knew, just so I could hear my own voice and, I hoped, coax better thoughts into my brain. "What you see here are inshore dolphins," I said. "The lab discovered there are three different social groups that migrate up and down the coast. They're all the same species, but they keep themselves separate. The inshore dolphins stay close to the land and travel partway up some of the rivers, where the water is still salty. Farther out there are near-shore dolphins, and beyond that the offshore dolphins—"

Turner interrupted me. "Uncle Alex," he said. "Could you put me down, please? I lost track."

I thought he'd lost track of what I was saying, so as I set his feet back on the deck, I began describing the three groups of dolphins once more, telling him that my colleagues hadn't yet figured out why the groups lived such different lives. I was going to explain a few of the theories, mention a bit about genetics and population dynamics, enough to pique his interest without confusing or boring him, but Turner didn't seem to be paying attention to me. He pointed at the closest group of dolphins. "I'll start over," he said, and then he was shouting out numbers again, bustling around the boat.

I wished I could start over, too. I walked to the helm and stood there, frightened, trying to convince myself that I really wasn't the kind of person who would ever drown his own nephew out of jealousy or anger or self-pity. As the gulls circled around us and as Turner kept finding more dolphins everywhere he looked, I told myself that the waking nightmare had been a passing impulse, gone now and best forgotten. My life wasn't leading up to something like that. I wouldn't allow it. Yes, it's true, Adrian and I might never learn how to talk with each other, let alone how to be friends. It had always seemed like such a waste to have but not have a brother. It still felt like a waste. I had to face that, and the distance that wouldn't disappear, and the damage already done. But none of it had to go any further.

I studied the water around us, made the count, wrote the numbers in the log, and prepared to move on. Before I restarted the engine, I called Turner over. He came and stood beside me. "This is great," he said.

I smiled and said, "Hold on tight."

I wanted him to be safe; I wanted him to have a wonderful time, and more than anything I wanted him to come back again and again. I waited until he had both hands wrapped around the grab rail. Then I pointed out toward the buoy that marked the site we had to visit next. I pushed the throttle forward and we began to accelerate. I shouted to Turner above the roar of the engine and the wind. I told him we had a lot more work ahead of us.

Drift

There wasn't another man and she knew her husband, Ronnie, was a decent, caring person and the sex was still satisfying, though a bit infrequent, and she loved her nine-year-old son, Leo, and she'd do almost anything to make him happy and she really had no detailed plan for the rest of her life, let alone the rest of the week. Nevertheless, for a while now Liz Ackerman had decided it was time for her to leave.

On the Friday she quit Survey Systems' phone bank, she came home earlier than usual. She found Ronnie standing in the kitchen of their apartment. He was wearing the dry-cleaned clothes he needed as deputy associate director of Haverford College's Human Resource Office: blue blazer, blue tie, white button-down shirt, khaki slacks. His face looked pink and smooth, as if he had shaved again during his lunch hour. "I tried to call you at work," he said. "They told me you had just been fired."

For at least the hundredth time, she was about to tell him it was all over, but she wasn't quite ready. She imagined telling him at night, in a quieter moment, in a somehow peaceful way. "I wasn't fired," she said. "I quit."

"I thought you were moving up. I thought you were making progress there."

"I could barely breathe in that room," she said. "Everyone talking at once, saying the same things over and over."

Ronnie stood by the refrigerator and poured himself a glass of ice water. He didn't look at her, just said what he always said these days: "Liz, you need a career."

"I know," she said. She told herself he'd be sorry later. He'd wish he'd appreciated her more and not taken her for granted. "What are you doing home so early?" she asked.

He drank the whole glass of water before answering. "The principal called about Leo again."

Liz sighed. "What did he do now?"

"The principal wants to discuss it with one of us in person."

"I'll walk over," Liz said. "I could use a walk. You go back to the office."

"I don't understand what's happening," Ronnie said. He set his empty glass on the counter and stepped toward Liz, as if he were about to hug her. Before he reached her, he stopped and looked down. "What's that in your hand?" he asked.

Liz followed his eyes and saw she was holding one of the headsets from Survey Systems. It was black, extremely light, and almost U-shaped, like a high-tech horseshoe.

"It's nothing," she said, moving the headset behind her back. "Did I tell you I stopped by Continental Drift the other day?

Gerard has an opening. He promised me a raise and my choice of shifts."

Ronnie walked past her, into the living room, and sat on the couch. "Gerard, Gerard," he said. "Of course he wants you. Still."

Gerard owned Continental Drift, which was her favorite restaurant, and she'd waitressed there for a while, before the phone bank and before the other recent jobs—in data entry and child care—that also hadn't worked out. During her waitressing days, she'd had a brief affair with Gerard, and after that ended she'd started spending time with Ronnie. She liked the work at Continental Drift, but she wasn't going to leave Ronnie to chase Gerard again. "It's not like that," she said.

"I don't want to hear it. No more waitressing, that's what we decided. And you'll have to return that telemarketing thing. You don't need them calling you a thief."

Liz put the headset on. She swiveled the little microphone up to her mouth. "May I speak with the man of the house, please?" she monotoned. "May I speak with the person responsible for making decisions?"

"You start somewhere," Ronnie said. "Then you move up."

He was making it easy for her, walking right into it. She could tell him how she wanted to move up, but not exactly in the way he was suggesting. Still, something held her back. She was remembering how Ronnie had looked during their early days together, before he'd started working at Haverford, when he was a part-time graduate student who painted houses and kept his hair tied in a ponytail. He'd show up at Continental Drift near the end of her shift, his clothes splattered with color, as if he'd been ambushed during one of those war games in the woods. He'd nurse a drink at the bar, waiting for her to close up and cash out. They liked to unwind with a few late night games of pool in a smoky lounge on City Line Avenue where the jukebox played only blues. Walking around the table, searching for the best shot, Ronnie often talked about studying physics someday. "I'd love to understand the laws of attraction," he said.

And the idea of moving up made her flash back to that day when, to celebrate six months of dating, they went for a ride in a glider. It was Ronnie's idea and he found the place, outside of Reading. A green and white Cessna towed them three thousand feet above the ground. Once they were released, the Cessna and its droning engine buzzed back down to earth. Their gaunt, bearded glider pilot flew them toward the Blue Mountains. Liz was shocked by how silently they sliced through the air. She couldn't speak. Ronnie tapped the pilot's shoulder. "Show us some maneuvers," he said. The pilot banked a few tight turns and then rolled them upside down. The Schuylkill River was beneath her head; the cloudless sky was above her clogs. Ronnie closed his eyes. Liz found her voice. "More," she said. "Take the stick," the pilot told her. "Ease it to the left." She did what she was told and the glider rolled upright again. They followed the river for a while. Liz pulled back to make them climb. She pushed forward to make them dive. "You could be good at this," the pilot said.

After they landed, she stepped down onto the grass runway, weak-legged and woozy. Ronnie knelt in front of her. She thought he was trying to get his balance back. Maybe he was about to boot. Then she heard what he was asking and she laughed. "Yes, honey," she said, "I'll marry you."

It had seemed like the perfect answer at the time. It was what she'd wanted then, she couldn't deny it, but how had her pony-tailed husband been transformed into the high-strung man slouched on her sofa? Was it Haverford? Fatherhood? Did it happen day by day or all at once? They were both thirty-five, but she had stayed more or less the same. Her curly black hair was untouched by gray. She kept herself trim. People at work told her she was looking better and better. She didn't believe them, but that was what they said. Meanwhile, Ronnie bought small rectangular bifocals, had his hair crew cut, and ran out of free time. Everyone at his office called him Ronald.

The tiny microphone still tilted toward her lips. "If I hadn't been a waitress," she said, "we never would have met."

"But we *did* meet," said Ronnie. "We're done meeting."

Yes, she could have said, you're absolutely right. We're done meeting. Instead, she joked around, telling herself that later would be better. It would be soon, though. She had to tell him soon. It was only fair. "You've been selected," she said into the microphone. "You may cancel at any time. Please answer the following questions. Does a member of your family own a dog or cat? A laptop? A power boat? A vacation home? A cellular phone?"

"There are other jobs, Liz. Leo's nine, but he'll be in college before we know it. We need to make more—"

"Does a member of your family wear eyeglasses? Smoke cigars? Work in a home office? How much would you be willing to pay for a humidifier with a space-age filtration system?"

Ronnie stood up. "Look," he said. "Give me that headset and I'll drop it off for you on my way back to the office."

Liz scrunched the headset into her pocket. "I'll take care of it," she said, and then she walked out.

OUTSIDE, ON THE EDGE of the Haverford campus in the middle of the still brightening May day, Liz strolled along the sidewalk, past buildings filled with students. There were shiny cars parked near the dormitories. Stereos blared. The college kids sprawled in lawn chairs with their shirts off, tanning for one party or another. They looked like models and movie stars. When the sun set and dinner time rolled around, some of them would be customers at Continental Drift. They were usually pleasant and easy to like. But they were also easy to resent. They were used to being served. They waltzed in, spent a small fraction of the money they had, tipped well, then sauntered off to spend more money around the corner.

For better or worse, that was the sort of future she pictured for Leo. He had the looks for it already, and he was sharp. She wanted him to star in school musicals, run unopposed for class president, win a dozen scholarships. Instead, he was developing what the principal, Dr. Jason Cave, called "a reputation." Sometimes she worried that her leaving might lead to Leo's reputation getting worse. Other times, though, she could almost convince herself that leaving might help him improve.

She was a half mile from the school when she saw a short, beer-bellied kid jump out of a pickup truck he'd driven right onto the sidewalk. He left the motor running and dashed inside. Liz watched him disappear into the building. She wondered what it would be like to take the truck. There it was, ready and waiting for someone capable of bold action. Without fear of consequences. So she walked toward it and climbed in. She had to pull herself up. The door was heavy and she used her whole body to shut it. The steering wheel was too close to her chest. She looked beside the seat for the controls. Her hands quivered and she kept glancing up to make sure the kid hadn't reappeared. She imagined lying to him. I've always wanted to drive a truck like this, she could say. Then she slid the seat back. Still no sign of the kid. Liz put the truck in gear and pulled out onto the street.

Speeding away, she checked the rearview mirror. No one was chasing her. She had never driven a pickup before and she liked being high above the road. She loosened her grip on the wheel. One at a time, she wiped her damp palms against her jeans. She needed to think carefully. She tried to guess how much the truck was worth and how much she could sell it for. She could use the money to finance the start of her new life. But she didn't know how to sell a stolen truck. She almost turned around, but she decided it would be safer to go on.

The Survey Systems headset was digging into her leg. She pulled it out of her pocket and tossed it onto the dashboard. Just as she reached the school, she passed a shaggy-haired jock on a periwinkle mountain bike. She saw him smile at her, so she took a hand off the wheel and waved. Then she parked in a distant corner of the lot, far away from the street.

WALKING ACROSS THE black asphalt toward the red-brick school, Liz focused on the tall glass windows and wondered where Leo was. In the first-floor classroom closest to the entrance, the kids looked like six- or seven-year-olds, too small for their desks. The teacher also looked very young, somewhere in her midtwenties. She seemed happy, writing bright yellow numbers onto a blackboard, and for a moment, Liz considered a career as a teacher. It could be a rewarding profession. There was still time to make a decision like that, though she would probably be the only truck-stealing teacher around.

Dr. Cave met her in front of his office and led her to a rigid, plastic chair that faced his desk. Then he asked his first question: "Is it true that Leo spends his evenings listening to John Lee Hooker?"

"I like John Lee a lot," she said.

The principal reclined in a brown, chief executive's chair, with a pillowy headrest and a matching ottoman. He flipped through several pages in a loose-leaf binder. His reading glasses were even smaller than Ronnie's. "Apparently, this is what occurred. During third period, Leo tossed two extremely chalky erasers at a classmate. When Mrs. Tismar asked what on earth he was doing, Leo said, 'Let this boy boogie-woogie, cause it's in him, and it's got to come out.' That's from 'Boogie Chillen,' if I'm not mistaken."

Liz smiled. "I'm impressed. You're not mistaken."

Dr. Cave turned to the next page in his binder. "That was not the only incident this morning, I'm sorry to say. During lunch period, Leo took the pink and green cardigan of Ms. Hax, our cafeteria attendant. He proceeded to put it on. When Ms. Hax told him to return her sweater, your son shimmied in what she called 'a crude fashion.'"

Liz tried to stifle a laugh, unsuccessfully.

Dr. Cave cleared his throat. "Although you seem to hold a different opinion, I believe this behavior needs to be taken seriously. It's important for you to realize that Leo's teachers describe this behavior as 'disrespectful,' 'disobedient,' and 'destructive.' They do not call it funny."

"I'm sorry for laughing, but there are worse things he could be doing, and I—"

"I'm not really interested in whether or not your son could engage in even more disruptive activities. I refuse to speculate. I simply hope he's at his worst now and that he will soon—*very* soon—begin to improve. That is what we strive for at this school. We are meliorists here. Everyone of us wants to better the hearts and minds of our children."

Liz wanted to be back in the pickup truck, driving away. She hoped no one had noticed it out there. She watched Dr. Cave set his binder and reading glasses on his desk. He rubbed the bridge of his nose with his thumb and forefinger. "Leo will sit in detention every afternoon for a week. In addition, for the remainder of this day, your son is suspended."

"He probably doesn't even know what he's doing," Liz said. "He's not a bad kid."

Dr. Cave looked younger without his glasses on. When he leaned forward, Liz wondered if he had children of his own. "Your son's a *good* kid," he said. "I *like* Leo. But he's doing bad things. Who knows where it could lead? I don't want to find out. I want these things to stop."

"Okay. I see what you mean. It's just that under the circumstances it's hard for me to—"

Dr. Cave waited for her to finish. "Is there anything else you want to tell me?"

If a different person had asked the same question, Liz might have found a way to go on, but instead she stood up. It felt good to leave that chair. "No," she said. "Not right now."

WHEN THEY APPROACHED the truck, Leo stopped and stared. "Cool vehicle, Mom," he said. "Is this ours?"

"Maybe," Liz said.

"Is it a present for Dad? He'll totally *love* it."

"Get in," she said, unlocking the door.

By the time she climbed behind the wheel, Leo was wearing the slim black headset. "Pilot to bombardier," he was saying. "Pilot to bombardier."

"Ha ha," Liz said. "Dr. Cave and I were just talking about what a funny little guy you can be. Now put your seat belt on. And give me that." She snatched the headset out of his ears and tossed it back onto the dashboard.

"Don't you want to hear my side?"

"Your side is in serious trouble," she said. He had once been sent to the principal's office for refusing to stop whistling during class. Back then, his dwarf defense—"I just wanted to whistle while I worked"—had helped him avoid punishment. Another time, he disappeared from gym and was later found in the music room, using the music teacher's stereo to blast an Elvis Presley CD. Then there was the afternoon he climbed onto the school roof during recess. Liz brought him home at the end of that day. Ronnie was waiting at the front door. "Are you training to be a sniper?" he'd shouted. "Is that the kind of son we're going to wind up with?" Leo tried to look tough, but he started to cry and he ran into the backyard. Ronnie went inside, shaking his head. "We're losing him," he muttered, as if their son were a heart patient about to flatline, not a kid who wanted more attention than he was getting.

But maybe Ronnie wasn't completely wrong. Before, the harshest punishment had combined a few group detentions with a lecture from an old ex-cop. Now Leo was suspended. Maybe the slippery slope started here. Liz could see that. Her son wouldn't be famous. Instead, he would be the notorious son of a notorious mother.

She drove out Lancaster Avenue, winding past Bryn Mawr and Villanova. The truck handled the curves well and Liz considered taking Leo on an educational tour for the rest of his suspension afternoon. She could warn him about what was coming while they visited Valley Forge Park and other famous places from the Revolutionary War. They could pick up some food for a picnic. But then she pictured the park police in their forest green uniforms. Did bringing stolen property onto a national historic site qualify as a federal crime?

She inhaled slowly, gazing through the big windshield, hoping the broad view would calm her, but she was wondering what kind of warning she could possibly offer. She looked over at Leo and saw that his brow was furrowed. She didn't want him to inherit her worries. She wanted to make his life better, not worse. She was a meliorist, too, in her own way.

"Mom, can I please tell you my side?"

"Sure, go ahead."

Leo explained that he threw the erasers after Brad Chilton

poked him twice with a freshly sharpened pencil. He showed her two tiny black dots on his forearm. "Brad wanted me to get lead poisoning," he said. "I tried to give him chalk lung."

"And what did Ms. Hax do to you?"

"She wouldn't let me shake my carton of chocolate milk."

"So, for that you swiped her sweater?"

"They were cheering behind me. Everyone loved it."

"Everyone didn't get suspended, though, did they?"

Leo fidgeted, reaching for the lock on the glove compartment.

"Leave that alone," Liz said. "I want to tell you something."

She watched Leo slip his hands beneath his thighs. He looked at his feet while she turned around in an immense gravel driveway. She knew she'd never make it as a car thief. She wouldn't make it as a principal or a father either. It would be a long list, if she really got started. Sometimes even being a mother felt far beyond her. "Mistakes are tricky things, Leo," she said. "You never know which ones will wind up hurting you."

They headed back in silence. When she pulled up in front of Ronnie's office building, she didn't cut the engine. She had more to tell Leo, but it could wait for now. "We'll hope this mistake is harmless," she said. "Now go keep your dad company. He might shout at you a little, but he'll be calmer here than at home. Tell him you'll do better in the future. And don't mention the truck."

She stayed behind the wheel and waited until she couldn't see her son anymore. Then she drove the pickup over to Continental Drift.

GERARD HAD DESIGNED the restaurant himself six-teen years ago. He'd renovated an 1890s, two-story boarding-house—upstairs he set up his office and workshop, downstairs the bar, kitchen, and dining room. It had been popular right from the start. The gimmick went with the name. The tables had been carefully carved into the shapes of continents and is-lands, though the scale was off. Parties of eight to twelve could sit comfortably around Asia, or they could slide South America and Africa together. Maps of all kinds hung from the walls. There were fossils, too, and a handful of seismographs in dis-play cases. The ceiling looked like a planetarium. The hardwood floors were painted foamy blue. The cuisine was advertised as international mish-mash.

Liz walked in just before five and a happy hour crowd had already gathered. Albert, the large, middle-aged bartender, was a rhino of a man. He waved when he saw her. She waved back and went upstairs, looking for Gerard.

Her short-lived, owner-employee affair during those pre-Ronnie days had featured a few fine breakfasts in the restau-rant kitchen—Gerard made a fabulous Hollandaise sauce for the eggs she scrambled with smoked salmon. While she stood at the stove, he would kiss the back of her neck. He was ten years older and she could feel those extra years in his hands, in the thickness of his fingers, in the palms he pressed against her hips. "Liz," he'd say, "why don't we do this more often?" She wondered the same thing. Then she'd come to work and he'd stay hidden behind his locked office door all night. She didn't think she was the only one knocking. After a month of that, she decided Gerard was dedicated to Continental Drift, and to Continental Drift alone. That's what she'd finally told him and he hadn't disagreed.

Now she found him hunched over his Singer sewing machine, patching the crotch of a pair of old blue jeans. Because he had the wind-lined face of a sailor, and because he liked to take charge, Liz sometimes called him Captain. Sketches of a new restaurant logo hung from the office walls. Gerard had been dreaming of opening another place for years. It would be called Plate Tectonics.

He jumped up and bear-hugged her. "Are you coming back to work?" he asked. Then he sat down on his sofa and patted the cushion beside him. "Talk to me," he said. "Tell me what's new."

Liz sat next to him. "Well, I didn't last in the telemarketing world. I quit before lunch today. Then I had a conference with Leo's principal. On my way there, I stole a pickup truck."

Gerard didn't say anything at first. He hooked his arm around her and peered into her eyes. "Say that last part once more."

Liz tried to stay casual about it. She shrugged her shoulders. "You ask what's new, you get what's new."

Gerard was on his feet again and he started pacing. "Actually, I don't get it at all. Is this something you planned? Is this that new career move you used to talk about?"

"It just sort of happened. I'm not sure what to do next."

Gerard sat back behind the Singer. He held up the jeans he was fixing. "I'll finish this while you give me more details. What did Leo do this time? Why did you quit? Does Ronnie know about this?"

Liz answered as best she could. She leaned forward, close to the edge of the sofa, her chin in her palms. She had to speak over the whir of the machine. She felt as if she'd been answering questions all day long. Or at least trying to.

Gerard paused in his work and stopped sewing. "Now tell me why you think you stole the truck."

The machine whirred again. Gerard used his hands to guide the denim and keep it taut. Liz watched his fingers push forward. He crouched over so far that his eyelashes almost brushed the stitches. "Well?" he asked.

"I stole the truck because it was running and I couldn't resist."

Gerard shook his head. "No," he said.

"I stole the truck because I wanted extra money."

"It's not about money."

"I stole the truck because I needed something new."

"Closer."

"Okay, Captain Freud. You tell me."

Gerard turned off the machine and snapped the threads with his teeth. He tossed the jeans onto his desk.

"Well?" she asked.

"Where is this truck as we speak?"

"It's behind the restaurant."

He started pacing again. When he passed Liz, he bent down, kissed her forehead, and kept moving. "Of course that's where it is," he said, "and I'll tell you why. You want me to climb into your flatbed. You want us to drive off together under the stars."

Liz laughed, even though she knew he wasn't far off. He just had the passenger list wrong. "Give me a break, Captain."

He looked her over. He tugged lightly on her sleeve. "A break," he said. "Grand theft auto and she wants a break! Here's what I've got at the moment. Your pants are fine. I have a shirt you can borrow and Nicole's been begging for the night off. You work dinner and I'll try to think of something to do with the stolen property. We all know the restaurant business is full of shady characters, right?"

"I wouldn't mind working," she said.

Gerard pulled a clean, white button-down oxford out of his closet and handed it to her. "I'll be downstairs," he said, and then he winked at her.

SHE MET HIM by the bar and he gave her a good group of tables. "All yours," he said, his arms open, ready for an embrace. Liz shook her head, walked by him, and settled right into a smooth rhythm. She had Australia, Greenland, Iceland, Japan, and Singapore. She pushed the steamed sausage and fennel dumplings, the high-alcohol ale brewed by Latvian monks, and the pear-apple cobbler with caramel gelato. As she took the orders and moved from the dining room to the kitchen to the bar and back, she could hear what Ronnie would say if he were standing by her side. "How does this beat working at a phone bank? Ferrying food instead of filling out forms? Repeating the same specials over and over? How is this any better?"

He'd probably come looking for her eventually, but she didn't want to think about that yet. Her tables were busy and she felt glad to be back, doing this temporary job. When her section got hammered hard between seven and nine, she handled it, and then she coasted. Throughout the night she showed how well she remembered her restaurant rap, sharing her knowledge of Gerard's peculiar dining room. It was a pleasure to have all the answers for a change. A customer asked her about the portrait on the cover of the menu. Who is that man in the Eskimo outfit? "It's Alfred Lothar Wegener," she said. "He's traveling through Greenland in that shot. He's the man who came up with the theory of continental drift." She pointed to the fossils from Brazil and Nigeria on the walls. "See how they match?" She told one couple a few names for the original land masses: Pangaea, Laurasia, Gondwana. A young boy, a baby-faced freshman with his parents, asked why there was no Atlantis table. Like a seasoned tour guide, Liz had her ready response: "Atlantis never was. The idea of large, sunken continents is geophysically impossible. Drifting, not foundering, explains it all." And she kept going. "Here's the real question," she said. "Here's something to study. What makes drifting happen? What is the driving force? That remains a subject of considerable debate."

After ten, the crowd thinned out and the kitchen began to close down. Liz wondered about her own driving force as she checked over her cash and receipts. Why the hell did I take that truck? she asked herself. She didn't want to speed off with Gerard, if he happened to be serious, which she doubted. He wasn't the answer. Did she need an answer right now? Couldn't she figure it out later? She stood in the wait station and gazed at the black-and-white photograph of Wegener that hung by the phone. He was smoking a hooked pipe, standing beside an Inuit guide. Both men were dressed head to toe in fur—their hands mittened, their faces almost completely hooded, their feet and calves wrapped in what looked like deep-shag carpet. She could make out a pair of igloos in the white behind them. Imagine a road trip to Greenland! Could she get there from here? Did they extradite? Did they even have police? She could follow in Wegener's footsteps. Like him, she could study the ice to learn exactly how the earth crashed and crumpled against itself every day.

Then she remembered that Wegener had died in Greenland. He froze alone on the way back to his base.

I should have thought this through before, she was telling herself, when two Japanese exchange students left their table and tried to carry chairs away from Asia. They had been quiet kids, until they started drinking. One had ordered the dumplings, the other had the Arctic char. Liz realized she should have cut them off after their first Latvian beer. Now they looked like they could be troublemakers. Was that how her son looked to the teachers at his school? A little menace? Another boy up to no good? Hoping that Ronnie hadn't been too hard on Leo, she stepped over to the Japanese kids. "What are you guys doing?" she asked.

"We're reclaiming the Kuril Islands," they both declared.

"Come on," she said. "You don't need to do this." She put her hands around the chair the dumpling guy was carrying. He was the thinner of the two, but he was stronger than she expected. She found herself in a tug-of-war, and she was losing. When she looked into her opponent's dark eyes, she felt like an extra in a martial arts movie.

"They belong to the emperor," the guy said.

"Give me a break," she said, trying to use her body weight to win.

A moment later, drawn off-balance, she tripped and found herself sitting on the blue floor, empty handed. Suddenly, the room seemed very quiet. Albert charged over from the bar. Face to face with him, the students looked like the harmless kids they were. They put the chairs down and began apologizing. "Sorry, sorry," they said. Liz stood up, thinking she would tell everyone not to worry about it. "You okay?" Albert asked. She brushed herself off, stretched her arms, rubbed her neck, and nodded. The last few diners went back to their food and their conversations. Before Liz could say anything, Albert was leading the kids away.

She caught up to them in the small alcove by the front door. Albert was seconds from bouncing both students out onto the street. Then Gerard joined them. He stepped between Albert and the kids. "Young men," he said, "tell me why you were taking those chairs."

"Let me throw these punks out," said Albert.

Gerard shook his head and waited. "Well?"

Liz was at his side. "It's all right, Gerard," she said. "They didn't mean it."

Gerard put a hand on her shoulder and watched the kids. Their backs were up against the door. The thin one spoke. "We were just joking around, mister."

"Good. Now tell me why you were joking around in my restaurant."

"We wanted to be funny," said the other kid.

Gerard shook his head again. "No."

The kid was surprised. "No?"

"I'll tell you why you took those chairs. You wanted attention. Now you've got it."

Albert cracked his knuckles. "Let me kick 'em out," he pleaded.

"They're sorry," Liz said. "They didn't really think it through."

Gerard kept staring at the kids. He raised an eyebrow, as if he were expecting something more from them. "What did they have?" he asked.

"Dumplings and the char," Liz said.

"Did they clean their plates?"

Liz was about to answer, but the thin kid beat her to it. "It was a feast," he said.

"Terrific food," the other kid said.

Gerard grinned. "You can go sit down," he said. "Order dessert if you want, but you'd better leave a good tip."

Liz watched them walk sheepishly to their table and return the contested chairs to Asia. Gerard started to massage Liz's shoulders. She let him. The whole episode had made her tense. She was arching her back into those hands when Ronnie walked in. She wasn't surprised to see him, but the poor timing startled her into silence. Gerard quickly removed his hands and put them in his pockets. "It's the restaurant hater," he said.

"What's going on here?" Ronnie asked.

"Your wife just prevented a brawl," said Gerard.

Liz worried that the exact opposite could be true if these two went at it. She was glad to see Albert turn away and lumber back to the bar. She watched Ronnie scan the dining room. Including the Japanese kids, there were six customers left. "Doesn't look like a rowdy crowd to me," he said.

"I hope you're right," Gerard said. Then he excused himself and walked up to his office.

Liz didn't know how best to begin. "Where's Leo?" she asked.

Ronnie stayed quiet and stared at her. He'd changed from

his work clothes and he was wearing blue jeans, a gray T-shirt, and a Haverford baseball cap, like one of the college kids. He looked away, took the cap off, ran a hand over his short hair, and said, "Are you leaving me?"

The first answer that flashed through her was, *Yes*. Was that all she'd needed? Someone to ask the question directly. Like a proposal, but the opposite. "Ronnie," she said, "let's sit down."

She led him over to a table and sat across from him. This late in the evening, with the lights dimmed, the dining room could feel like a luxury liner, churning along on the open sea. The stars in the ceiling shimmered. With a little imagination, the clatter of dishwashing and table clearing became the slap of surf against their ship. Ronnie kept glancing toward the stairs.

"Can I get you anything?" Liz asked.

"No, thanks," he said. He reached over and tugged the cuff of her shirt. "Is this one of Gerard's?"

She pulled her arm away. "It's a work shirt. I borrowed it. It's been a real strange—"

"Look. Leo didn't know where you were and I've been driving all over. He said you had something to tell me, so just tell me."

She leaned back in her chair, picturing Leo trying not to mention the truck. "Leo and I were talking about something else. Give me a minute and I'll try to explain everything. You sure I can't get you a drink?"

"I'm sure. You waitress, I'll wait. Like the good old days."

"I'll be right back," she said. She walked over to the Japanese kids, who were quietly finishing their beers. They didn't want dessert, so she gave them their check. Then she went to tip out Albert. He was talking to a young woman who must have just come in from a full day at the spa. Wearing a lavender sundress, glass beads, and sandals, she glowed by the bar. Was this the waitress who'd needed the night off? She'd probably used the free time for aromatherapy and herbal wrapping.

"Is Gerard around?" the woman asked.

Albert pointed to the stairs.

"Have fun," Liz said.

The woman smiled and walked up toward the office. Liz caught the scent of jasmine. When she heard the door open, shut, and lock, she was briefly tempted to leave the truck at the restaurant and call the cops, but she didn't doubt that Gerard would turn her in. She gave Albert his cut and asked for two bottles of the Latvian ale, which she carried back to the table.

"For the road," she said, giving one of the bottles to Ronnie. "There's a surprise outside."

Just then, the two Japanese kids came by. The thin one handed her a stack of bills. "Thank you very much," he said. They both bowed low from the waist, arms rigid at their sides.

Liz chuckled. "Cut that out," she said to them. "Go on and enjoy the rest of your night."

The two students straightened up and marched toward the door. Ronnie took a sip from his bottle. "You're better at this than I remember," he said.

LIZ HAD PARKED the truck between a Dumpster and the head cook's motorcycle. "You really stole this?" Ronnie asked. "You actually stole it?"

"Shh," Liz said.

Ronnie took a few swigs from his bottle of ale. "All right," he said. "I'm surprised."

Liz leaned against the driver's side door. It seemed so solid, cool against her back. "It was there and I took it," she said. "I don't know what came over me."

One of the busboys walked out and dropped three bags of garbage into the Dumpster. "Nice truck," he said.

"It's not ours," said Liz.

"It's still a nice truck," the busboy said, heading inside again.

Liz wanted him to hang around. Maybe he could offer some sort of advice or support. But he was quickly gone and she could feel Ronnie staring at her. "You are leaving me, aren't you?" he said. "How else am I supposed to understand this?"

She wanted to have her reasons ready. She wanted to be able to tell him that it was more than a feeling she had, more than something she believed she had to do. And she also wanted to decide for herself when to tell him. She didn't want to be forced into it. So she stepped around it again. "Did you give Leo a hard time at the office?" she asked.

Ronnie waited, as if he were giving her a chance to say more. Noise drifted out from the restaurant. Whoever was mopping in the kitchen sloshed a bucket of water onto the floor. Someone was playing Bob Marley. And, almost on the beat, there was a woman's voice, moaning. It could have been part of the music, but it was coming from Gerard's office. The captain was sailing on, as usual.

Ronnie stopped waiting and said, "Sure, okay, let's talk about Leo. That's a logical topic of discussion. You said you were going to pick him up; then you can't even take care of him for an afternoon. No, you need to rush off. You need to cover a shift for old Gerard." Ronnie crossed his arms, as if to hold himself back. He looked up into the sky and exhaled. "To answer your question: Leo and I did our work. We went out for pizza. When he fell asleep, I took him next door and drove over. Leo's going to be fine."

"I'm worried about him," Liz said. Then she laughed. "Listen to me. I'm worried about myself, too. Today the principal treated me as if I were contagious." She pushed herself away from the truck. "I guess I'm worried about everything."

"I answered your question," Ronnie said. "Can you answer mine?"

She braced herself for his reaction, watching him closely. He looked calm and composed, waiting for her to say the words so he could start to deal with them. He was daring her to go ahead. It was late at night and they were standing by her stolen truck and he was clearly pissed off and tired and she'd made him find her at their first meeting place, a place he'd grown to hate, and yet she saw that he was going to be efficient. All business. She kept her hands at her sides, not wanting to touch him. Still, she wanted to rattle him. She wanted to shake his confidence on her way out. Was it as simple as that? "Yes," she said. "I can answer your question. And, yes, I'm leaving."

It took Liz a few months to realize that somewhere in the back of her mind she'd expected Ronnie to argue with her. To plead for another chance. Maybe even sink to his knees, promise to change, and beg her to stay. But nothing like that

happened, not then, not during the slow, steady divorce process that followed, and not during the years of shared custody
that saw Leo mature into a successful scholarship student at
Haverford.

"I care less than you think," Ronnie said. Then he turned his
back on her, and without another word he walked away. His
shoes kicked up pieces of loose gravel from the parking lot. He
held his head high as he stepped quickly into the restaurant and
out of sight.

Liz didn't stand there long. She gave him fifteen minutes
to come back to her, then twenty, then she checked her watch
again and climbed into the truck. She didn't have a plan, but
she'd take care of first things first. She reached across the dashboard, grabbed the Survey Systems headset, and pitched it into
the Dumpster. Then she started the engine and revved it up
before driving out of the lot. There wasn't much traffic on the
roads as she made her way to the college. She watched her speed
and the drivers she passed looked like they were also being cau-
tious, probably taking it slow because they'd had a few drinks
while they were out. Maybe they'd wandered a bit during the
evening, maybe they'd strayed, but they hadn't drifted too far.
They hadn't stolen anything. They hadn't ended a marriage.
They leaned close to their steering wheels, peering through
their windshields, hoping to get home safe.

She wasn't going home. She was taking the truck back where
she'd found it. When she drove past the dormitories the stereos weren't blaring as loudly as they'd been earlier, but there
was still music to be heard and she could see students dancing
and drinking by more than one window. Then she pulled up in

front of the building where she'd seen the beer-bellied kid rush inside. The place looked quiet. She turned off the truck, set the keys beside her on the seat, and opened the door.

She didn't want to be seen, and as far as she could tell she wasn't. A car sped past while she climbed down onto the sidewalk. She turned away from the headlights and walked off into the darkness, swinging her arms like she was a law-abiding citizen out for a healthy evening stroll, but she couldn't stop herself from looking back. She kept expecting to see that beer-bellied kid, sprinting toward her, shouting, demanding to know why she'd stolen his truck. She would try to explain it all to him. How her life would be different from now on. How it would be better. And she was ready to say she was sorry. She was prepared to ask for his forgiveness. She listened hard for his footsteps and she looked back again and again, but there was no one running after her, no one demanding a single thing of her.

Proposals and Advice

I.

Eric, our grandchild, our number one and only, so much like a son to my wife Milly and me, has called to say he will come to visit next weekend. He'll want advice, some life knowledge and wisdom to take away with him, but at my age, with the way my mind works, I don't know if I can be of much help and I find myself thinking of my father.

My father died when I was nine, but before that there were days when he would come home from work, open the front door, and find me alone in the living room, doing my assignments for school. My mother would be out back in the garden, or down the street, checking in with the other mothers of our

Philadelphia neighborhood. So, since I was the one right there, waiting and attentive, my father would tell me about his day, talking to me as if I were old and wise enough to comprehend what he had to say.

Long before the days of charge cards, my father had made himself into the local equivalent of Visa or American Express, minus the exorbitant interest rates and annual fees. He once had other occupations, but after he immigrated to Philadelphia from the shores of the Black Sea, he mastered the language of the city, and twenty-two years old, he struck up relations with a number of large department stores, negotiating cut rates in exchange for bulk business. He would spend his days walking from building to building, offering other immigrants the chance to buy whatever they wanted on installment, month by month.

Often, when he talked to me those days in the living room, he would take off his jacket, untie his shoes, and complain. He knew firsthand the strain of coming to a new country and starting a new life, and it pained him to see people purchase what they couldn't afford. "You know, Charlie," he'd say, "I have advice and wisdom because I've been around. I try my best to give it away for nothing. For free. But too many people want only what will cost them. Wait, I tell them, wait until you've been married, wait until the baby is more grown. What's the rush? You don't need such a big, expensive appliance now. You don't need fur, such fine shoes, jewelry. But they don't listen to me. I tell them I know. I tell them it will cost them nothing to take my word for what I say." Then my father would pause, for effect, looking into my eyes, trying to make certain that I, his own flesh and blood, would hear and heed his words: "Everybody wants, but not what I have to give away."

In the end, no matter what he thought, he couldn't say no, because they'd just go through his old partner, Hess, or someone else, and he knew, and we knew, that at least he would be forgiving, letting his customers take as long as they needed, letting payments go if they had to go, because that's what he did. If someone asked for more time, he'd give them that. And he didn't lord his warning over them. "It's not for me to tell them I told them," he'd tell me.

Not yet ten years old, I didn't understand much of what my father meant. Still, I listened and looked up at him when he spoke.

In the seventy-odd years I've lived since then, I've often longed to hear my father's advice, longed to see him appear before me again, vivid and so certain. It's dying young, I've come to believe, that let him keep his confidence. He came across the ocean alone, made himself a successful life in an unknown land, and then, before doubts, old age, and powerlessness could settle onto his shoulders, he passed away, sure of everything he knew.

RECENTLY, ON HIS thirtieth birthday, Eric found himself suddenly unsure about everything. On the phone, he told Milly and me what happened, but his account seemed to be missing details. My imagination went to work, filling out the fragments. I pictured him up north in his Boston apartment, with Dr. Laura Ninnovich, who was a pediatric resident, his girlfriend of the past seventeen months, and the woman he knew he would love for the rest of his life. He was just where he wanted to be, in bed beside her. He woke up early, waiting for the sun to rise, which it did, the last thing that went as he expected, orange light brightening the room, sparkling across Laura's hair, across her tan runner's legs.

He had a plan, already well started. He stepped into the bathroom to clean himself up. Then he sneaked into the kitchen, removed the bottle of champagne hidden in the lettuce drawer, grabbed the roses stored beneath the sink, and made his way back to the bed. He took a small, velvety box from his night table drawer, held it in his hand as he kissed Laura lightly on the lips to wake her up.

She knew what day it was, and moving close to him with a hug and kiss in return, she softly said, "Happy birthday, Eric," nuzzling her head against his chest.

Eric said, "Do you know what I want for my birthday?" but she was still sleepy. She mumbled something about time, to him, or in a dream, and he said, "Listen. This is sort of important."

"Uh-uh," she said.

He considered slowing down, he thought about waiting, but I imagine he kept going, according to plan, saying, "I want to give you this," as he set next to her head, before her almost closed eyes, the small jewelry box.

Up she sat, placing the box in the palm of her left hand, opening with her right, and here he did wait, at least for a few seconds, watching her eyes. Then, with his voice full of certainty, Eric said, "Laura Ninnovich, will you marry me? Will you marry me, Laura Ninnovich?"

She was suddenly very awake, admiring the ring, and a pause came, all wrong. He knew first from her breathing, the way there was no gasp of pleasure, only the holding of breath, as if she wanted time to stop, as if she wanted to stay still in the space between her heartbeats, use the quiet to think of the right, gentle words to say.

But, really, she had probably thought it through, stood far ahead of him, saw it coming, sensed for months now that she would have to tell him, No. I can't.

They talked for a while in his bed, champagne and roses useless on the floor, and Eric became the one who wanted time to stop, to turn back, so he could keep this from happening, and he hardly heard Laura say that she knew they would have to break up or get married, that she was not ready to marry, that she had planned to break up. He thought about asking questions, asking, Why why why, but then his time did turn back, and his mind filled with the night before, how he went from his office to Laura's hospital, and they walked back to his apartment and made love moving from the couch to the carpet to the wing chair and then they showered and went out for Cajun food, ordering spicy dishes—blackened, Tabascoed, hot peppered—but he tasted none of it because he was leaning back in his chair, looking across the table at the woman he had definitely wanted to marry since the day, running alongside the Charles, he found her, and he could sense only her, nothing but her; she was twenty-nine, he was a few hours from thirty, the two of them so young, fit, and fortunate, destined for decades together. And she had glanced up, catching his eyes in hers, saying, "What are you thinking about over there?" as he sat quietly, just breathing and smiling, while she shortened the question, asking, smiling back, "What?"

Eric could not speak, but he knew in the morning he would, and he could see the answer he desired in everything about her.

• • •

WHEN HE CALLED, he told us how he had been driving through the Berkshires for a few days, and is it any wonder? He spent hours and hours searching for where he went wrong, thinking his timing must have been off, he should have waited until the evening, or let her brush her teeth first, or chosen a Saturday instead of a Wednesday. Other words, other scenarios, completely different ways of proposing ran through his tired mind until at last he decided he should spend some time at home, so he called.

He's a good boy, our number one and only, and we're always proud of him. He's smart, received his PhD, though not in a subject you would respect right off the bat, not engineering or economics or chemistry—he is a doctor of English. Which, even he acknowledges, from my perspective, is a pretty odd thing. My father, for example, when he came across from Russia, all on his own, learned English, and then he met a woman he loved, and he taught her, and together they taught me. Nobody needed a PhD to teach and learn to speak what filled the world around them. You were going to stay quiet? You were going to work only with people who spoke Yiddish or Russian?

I'm Eric's *zayde,* the closest thing to a father he has, and I want to be able to give him sage advice. I want to be able to speak words Eric can use to solve the problems he has to face. I want to feel, like my father before me, that after all these years I've accumulated so much valuable knowledge that what I say overflows with answers. But, instead, when I search for advice to offer, for wisdom and insight, I discover only anecdotes—my mind drifts back into the past, recalling what happened when, who said what to whom.

I know about marriage; I know about a love that lasts from decade to decade, passes half a century, and goes on. I know, also, what it is to lose a father. I do. But maybe I don't know enough. There's always more than I can understand.

II.

Milly believes she understands Eric's current problems completely. She blames everything on our daughter Barbara, Eric's mother, who is off who knows where exactly. It is the obvious connection to make, but I probably should explain as best I can what she means, about Barbara and her ill-suited suitor, her flimflam fiancé, her hopeless husband, Leonard Lutz.

Go back to a Sunday morning, decades ago, in this very house, in our bedroom, Barbara running in, all of twenty years old, waking us up to share the story of the proposal that had come her way.

We listened until the end, until Barbara was out of breath, extending her arm toward us so that once we wiped the sleep from our eyes, we'd be able to see the size and beauty of the diamond ring on her finger. The hand dangled before us, as if it were waiting to be kissed. Milly looked into the green eyes of our daughter and asked, "Where is Mr. Leonard Lutz right now?"

"He left."

"Did you just say he left?"

"Yes, yes, he left."

"Well," Milly said, getting out of bed, revealing her red

flannel pajamas, putting her feet into her slippers and brushing away the ringed hand from before her. "If he doesn't come back for fifty years, long after I'm dead and decaying beneath the ground, it will be too soon."

Barbara stood there, not knowing what to do, shocked, as was I. It wasn't the finest engagement story; it was not at all difficult to imagine better. Still, I was willing to take a look at the ring and wait for Leonard to come back around to answer questions. But Milly's mind was made up and she wanted to resolve the situation immediately.

"That man is not for you, Barbara," she said. "It's obvious. You give that ring right back to him. You don't know how it pains me to see this. Here, let me take that ring off your finger right now."

Barbara snapped back her hand and ran out of the room, slamming the door behind her.

Even then, nearly thirty-two years ago, Milly could not move very quickly, but her mind never fell behind. Although she did not give chase that morning, she knew that our daughter was in the process of making a mistake, a mistake that resulted from a thinking slowed and clouded by the desire to be in love. She turned and looked at me sitting there, staring at our closed door. "That boy Leonard," she said. "I'm not happy about him at all. He doesn't even know his own mind."

"She's not going to give that ring back," I said.

"Not today, maybe. But when she does, sometime in the time to come, she'll wish she had done it sooner."

As usual, Milly was right. Two years and two months later, a year after giving birth to Eric, Barbara did return the ring, just before she ran away again, and farther.

Here's the unorthodox way in which Leonard proposed to our daughter, as she told us herself, uncritical in her momentary happiness: to celebrate a year and a half of casual dating, of meeting for movies, for meals, for drives away from the city, Leonard took Barbara downtown for an Italian dinner on a Saturday evening. He was twenty-four at the time; she was twenty. After dinner, as they drank coffee and shared a piece of cheesecake, Leonard said they needed either to break up or get married. Barbara was surprised and had no idea exactly what to expect, but she bravely agreed. "Let's break up," he said. Again, she agreed, then she walked out, found a cab to take her home, and slipped silently into her room.

She didn't sleep well. She barely slept at all and the next morning she was in the kitchen before dawn, making coffee. She was trying not to think about Leonard's face, his puffy red lips, so much softer than her own. Then she heard his voice, whispering, "Barbara, let me in." She worried that she'd drifted into a waking dream, but the voice didn't go away and when she looked out the window, she saw him standing right there, and though she was wearing only her nightgown and bathrobe, she opened the door for him and he was speaking quickly, talking about having been walking all night; it grew darker, he said, he could not believe how dark, and he could not stop thinking. "I changed my mind," he said. "We should marry." And while she watched, he took her hand and placed the ring on her finger. She looked at the narrow band of gold and the glittering diamond and she felt thrilled and exhausted at the same time. She didn't know how to respond. All she knew was that she no longer wanted coffee. Instead of inviting him inside, she said good night, closed the door, returned to her room, and fell asleep for a few hours. It was well after sunrise when she awoke again and ran into our room.

"Marriage proposals," Milly said, "should not be surrounded by uncertainty. Forethought is required. A man who doesn't know for sure whether he wants to get married or get broken up—"

"When I proposed," I reminded her, "I didn't know what I was doing."

"Maybe that's true, but you didn't tell me that. You didn't take me out to dinner and say, Milly, I don't know what I'm doing. No, you said, 'Milly you drive me crazy and I want to marry you.'"

When Barbara did eventually do what Milly had said she would one day do, she also decided that she wanted to move to California and begin a new life by herself, without Eric and without us. I did my best to intercede because, of course, I love my daughter, but also, I suppose, because I was not ready to care for a one-year-old at that time in my life. I went to Barbara in her room, where she was gathering her things, and I asked her to stop packing. I told her I could introduce her to some nice young men and she packed faster. I said I'd help her find an apartment for herself, nearby, and I'd contribute for expenses, and we'd be great, convenient, inexpensive baby-sitters, and really, there was no reason to run all the way out to California where no one could ever see her. But her mind was made up. She married when she wanted, had a child when she wanted, divorced when she wanted, and started over when she wanted. As much as she would like to see herself as different from her mother, I know she is the same. I know that when they make up their minds, there is nothing anyone can say, especially me.

More than that, though, I believe Barbara is my father's granddaughter, blessed or cursed by the impulsiveness that pushed and pulled him to another world. What would it have been like to know him as a young child, not yet a man? To watch him pack up his meager belongings in the middle of the night? How straight he would have stood. How unblinking his eyes. Who would dare to dissuade him? And who would not hope for his return, to see him come home again a success, grown, his promise met and surpassed?

In the end I could only watch my daughter go.

WITH THAT SORT of background, Milly would say, it's not at all surprising that Eric took dating very seriously. He didn't want to make his parents' mistakes. He would know exactly what he wanted and he would ask for it directly. So he wouldn't fiddle and so he would be prepared, Milly gave him for his twenty-fifth birthday the diamond from one of her mother's earring heirlooms to use in an engagement ring. But where did all Eric's carefulness get him? Broken up himself. Milly and I have met Laura and we like her. She's no female Leonard Lutz, and we were willing to feel, with Eric, that she was the one who would bear our great-grandchildren. So what do we know, after all? How can we trust whatever advice we decide to offer?

III.

Sometimes I sense that Milly and I have become too accustomed to loss, making us perhaps not the best people to help Eric through his sadness. We've lived too long. Time passes and we let piece after piece of our lives slip away. Just as our parents learned English because it filled the space around them, we have learned how to relinquish because we must. There seems to be more and more that lies beyond our control—friends and family we've known for decades pass away, or their minds go, or a cancer eats away at them and we are powerless, unable to offer real help. We can only comfort as best we can those who are leaving and those who are left behind.

Depending on the day of the week, we can be found swimming, walking, bowling, doing what we can to keep our bodies from falling apart, but that too is beyond our control. Without the valves of a pig that have been sewn into my heart, I would have been dead for more than a decade. Inside Milly's body, there is an artificial hip and a pacemaker they adjust from time to time. When we sit down to eat, we set before us a small, bright rainbow of pills. Some might see hope in those colorful capsules and tablets, some might see neatly packaged scientific triumphs, cures for what was once incurable. And there is that, I must admit. But for us the pills are also reminders of past and future troubles.

I'm sure Eric did not want to make me feel old and close to an end; he couldn't have known that his return and need for advice would make me think about the past that will disappear with Milly and me. What I try to keep in mind is that loss, as impending as it is and will be from now on, actually unites the three of us, the grandparents and the grandson, the *bubba*, the *zayde*, and the number one. And I suppose that's part of what I want to let Eric know.

So I search for pronouncements, but instead of a clear lesson what enters my mind is a sunny afternoon, a little more than six years ago. Milly was sitting in the living room, innocently practicing on the piano, when suddenly half of her world went dark.

IT WAS AS IF, she came to say, a black curtain had been dropped down. The metronome was on, clicking from side to side, and the change, complete, took not even a beat. She wondered if perhaps her right eyelid had somehow become stuck. "Something's happening," she said. "Charlie, Charlie, something's happening."

I was sitting in my blue reading chair in the corner of the room, looking at the paper. I jumped to my feet, too fast, and my world grew blurry, as it does when I try to move quickly. My heart needs time to pump my blood where it needs to go.

"What is it?" I asked, walking slowly toward her, letting the room come back into focus. I said, "Let me see," and I was frightened, remembering my own experience from years ago, how I slipped from the conversation and a friend wisely hustled for the phone. A stroke, I thought. A stroke. Milly's having a stroke.

We were both scared, but she was staying calmer than I could. She stood up beside the piano. She stopped the clicking of the metronome, closed the keyboard cover, and rested her hand there. "It's my right eye," she said.

For years, Milly has been wearing contacts, almost since they first became available, and she spoke exactly the way she did when she had dropped or couldn't find one of her lenses, her voice empty of panic. She covered her left eye with her hand and opened her right eye wide. "There's nothing," she said. "Not blurry. Just dark."

"Let me see," I said again, and with my hand I took her hand from her eye. "Is it only the eye? You're not feeling faint? Dizzy? You don't think this is a stroke, do you?"

"It's nothing like that, honey, but can you see anything there?"

I could see both contacts in place. There was nothing in or over her eye that I could make out, but the color of it did seem to have faded slightly. "It looks fine. Are you sure you're not dizzy? Do you feel confused?"

"No, no," she said, "but I'm going to keep my eyes closed until we see a doctor." Then she took my arm. It was as if she wanted to practice being blind, so she'd be prepared. I wanted to tell her that it was a silly idea, that she could see fine out of her left eye. But what did I know? Whatever logic was operating, if any was operating at all, was far beyond me. For all I knew, keeping her eyes closed might be the perfect thing to do; it could save her sight, bring back her right eye and preserve her left. In the future, we could find ourselves sitting on the back porch, talking to friends, telling the story of how the decision to keep her eyes closed saved her life. "Okay," I said, and I led her out to the car.

• • •

IN THE EMERGENCY ROOM, the first doctor had no idea what the problem was. Milly opened her eyes, and sight was still in the left, gone from the right. The doctor's main questions were about blood pressure. He wanted to know if she had been upset or very excited, with her heart beating quickly before her vision slipped away. She shook her head. "I was playing the piano, a slow song. It's my husband here who has the real heart problems."

We were directed across the hospital, to the eye clinic. The doctor didn't want Milly to exert herself further, so she sat in a wheelchair and I pushed her down the corridors, into and out of the large elevator. Milly looked at me and then closed her eyes again. The doctor had said she could keep her eyes open, that it would be fine to do that. "Do you know exactly what's wrong?" she asked him. "Do you know what's happening to me here?"

"No," said the doctor. "Not exactly. Not yet."

"I'll keep my eyes closed for the time being then," she said, "if you don't mind."

And then she was taken away, and I waited alone. Personally, I don't like to sit down in hospitals, but Milly won't tolerate pacing. I think that if you sit there and wait long enough, something will go wrong with you, too. People die and it's not unimaginable that what afflicted them needs to go off and find a new person, so it floats through the air toward those who are waiting. I keep moving, I walk and walk, and I long to leave. I paced the eye clinic waiting room, unnerving those around me, I'm sure, but my mind was elsewhere.

• • •

WHAT THE EYE SPECIALIST knew with certainty was that sight would not be coming back to her right eye. He also knew, he said, that there was definitely nothing wrong with her left eye.

Milly and I were silent. For those of our generation it is no easy thing to challenge the authority of doctors. They still have a certain power over our health and we don't want to offend them. We don't believe in second opinions. We don't believe we're getting opinions in the first place. But I wanted answers, so after a pause I rattled off some questions. "Will she have to wear a patch over her eye?"

"Only if she wants to."

"Can she drive?"

"Eventually, if she wants to."

"How does she need to adjust her life at this moment?"

"She will lose peripheral vision on her right side so she will have to turn her head more, use her neck."

And in the months and years that followed, her left eye remained strong. But because she was not accustomed to turning her head so often, she tripped stepping from a curb and broke her hip, which makes bowling slightly more difficult, but it has not stopped her at all.

The side effect that the doctor did not come close to anticipating, but that I should have predicted, had to do with the increased power that accompanied this loss of vision. Yes, she had to be more careful moving around. But at the same time she had an irrefutable argument for traveling. She would say where she wanted to go. I would say, No, we can't possibly go there—we don't have enough money—and I've heard terrible things about that place. Then we would go back and forth, about money, about who said what and why they said it until eventually Milly would say, ending the discussion and absolutely winning her way, "I've lost one eye already, and who knows how much longer the other will last, and this is something I want to see before I can't."

So she's lost some of her vision, but before our first trip after the loss, we went shopping for a monocular, and she picked out a small device she can wear around her neck on a chain. Since then she has pointed her monocular at the temples of Kyoto, the bald eagles of Alaska, the pyramids of Egypt.

Oftentimes, though, when she's not using the monocular—and this epitomizes what makes me follow her always—I catch her looking at me. I remember as we were leaving the hospital that evening, after we had signed a few more papers, I asked Milly why she tried so hard to keep her eyes closed through so much of the day. "Did you really think that you could keep the sight from slipping away if that's what it was going to do?"

"I don't know," she said. "I don't know. But I did know that if I was going suddenly to stop seeing, I wanted my last sight to be of you."

WHAT WILL ERIC DO when I tell him that? And when I tell him about my father? What will he hear? Will it make any difference?

I worry about what to say, about how to help, but it's not only the big questions that baffle me. I also wonder what we have in the refrigerator, how we'll spend each day, how long he'll stay.

Should we drive out to the Jersey shore? Should we go downtown for a concert at the Academy of Music? Flea markets? Movie matinees? Bowling?

I don't know enough, I'll tell him. I haven't done enough, and I never will. I certainly do not deserve the gift of being the last sight my wife would choose to see.

It's the people I've stood alongside, I'll say. Listen.

And then, to wrap it all up, neat and clear, I'll try somehow to explain that it's been my greatest fortune to have been loved by those close to me, though I have no idea how or why.

That should take thirty minutes. Maybe forty-five if I speak slowly and let myself be interrupted. And the visit will just be starting.

Eric will want something else when he steps through our front door, but I can't bring Laura back to him; I can't make her change her mind. I can't even make Barbara, my own daughter, pick up the phone, call home from time to time.

No matter what, though, right up until the end, I can keep talking.

Maybe my father was a peddler of advice as well as of appliances and I was just too young to know that he knew no more than I know now. Maybe he said everything when he complained that you can never fully understand the needs and wants of others. Maybe, finally, loss is all we can count on.

Nevertheless, over the years, I've often been amazed by the details that come hurtling back to me about those late afternoons I spent together with my father in the living room. What has been lost is not necessarily gone. Sometimes I'll wake up in the morning and a whole conversation will have returned to me in the night, as if my father had spoken to me while I dreamed. Or I'll be walking down the street, or visiting the neighbors, and suddenly I'll have before me a brilliant picture of the hat he wore, its texture, its color, the bend of the brim, the tilt it had on his head, and the slow motion with which he took it off, set it in his lap, as he sat beside me to tell me about his day.

Eric's driving toward us on his zigzag path, haunted and saddened by the memories he cannot forget—the feel of her skin, the look in her just-opened eyes, the roses, the champagne, the offered ring. He's coming down from the Berkshires, past the Finger Lakes of upstate New York, through the coal-mining Lackawanna Valley of Pennsylvania, and he wants to leave behind Laura and everything about her—he wants it all out of his mind.

But I wish my grandson, my number one and only, were already here, by my side. Remember it all, I'll tell him. Someday you'll want those memories, every one of them.

Reunion

Scott didn't understand his sister, Kim. She should have arrived hours ago. She was bringing her third husband, Jacob, and they'd all planned to meet in the afternoon at the hospital. The weather could have caused delays—it was early December in Philadelphia, the city awash with cold, brown slush—but Kim hadn't called. The afternoon came and went. The sun set. Scott didn't eat dinner until almost ten, hoping Kim would make it in time. She didn't. At eleven, Scott was home, still waiting.

He sat on the living-room couch with his wife, Claudia. He opened a bottle of chablis and remembered the last time he'd seen his sister. Months ago at a cousin's wedding in Boston. Kim and Jacob had threatened to dance right through dinner. Kim kept joking about how she was trying to get pregnant, how dancing was supposed to help.

Scott turned to his wife and saw the sad, long day in her face—dry skin, chapping lips, circles beneath her eyes. He surely looked worse. Eight hours in the hospital, sitting there and knowing that his mother would never be the same again. She had pancreatic cancer. There was before the surgery and then there would be after the surgery. She'd beaten breast cancer years earlier, when she was sixty-two, but there was no beating this one. Still, as she checked into the hospital, she'd said, "I'll go through this with style. This is old hat to me. I'll be an extraordinary patient."

Scott heard her voice catch at the word *patient*.

Even Tommy, Scott's six-year-old adopted son, had sensed something passing away during visiting hours. Standing by her bed, he'd slipped into silence, staring hard at his grandmother in the strange room, as if he were using all his energy to remember where she was and how she looked.

On the couch, Scott sighed and poured the wine for Claudia.

"I might need something stronger," she said. She drank off half the glass.

"Let's get through this first." He poured her glass full again and put his arm around her. "Tommy must know what's happening," he said. "He was so quiet today."

"If only he had a brother or sister," she began. Then she stopped herself and drank more wine. "I wonder where Kim and Jacob are."

"Who knows. All I know is I'm not ready for this."

"You can never be ready."

"Mom told me about her stomachaches weeks ago. I told her to take Metamucil."

Claudia rested her free hand on his thigh. "You have nothing to feel guilty about, Scott. This is something that's happening. It's not your fault."

"Maybe Kim's not coming at all," he said. "Maybe she and Mom had another fight."

He could recall plenty of humdingers. Some of the fights went on for years. When his mother criticized Kim during the first divorce, Kim stopped speaking to her for eighteen months. She didn't grow more understanding when their father died. One afternoon, two weeks after the funeral, Scott had watched Kim clean out his mother's refrigerator. It started when she reached in for milk. She wound up stacking plastic-bagged leftovers on the counter, complaining about the stink. "How can you live like this?" she snapped. Her back straight, her face hard, her hands moving fast. She bit her words out into the world: *pitiful, disgusting, pathetic, ridiculous.*

Claudia poured him more wine. "She fought with your father, too, didn't she?"

"All the time. Right up to the end."

"I don't know," Claudia said. "I guess it's easier to talk about her than your mother."

"I'm not ready for Mom to be dying."

Claudia massaged the back of his neck. "How did Kim sound when you talked with her?"

"Normal. Rushed. Who knows. Maybe she wants to wait until everything is over before she shows up."

At last there was a knock on the door and Scott stood to let his sister in. On the threshold, she looked somehow untouched, as if she had come straight from a workout, giving off a healthy glow. But when he stepped closer he noticed a patch of eczema on her neck and acne beneath the makeup on her cheeks.

"Kimmy," he said, midhug, "where have you been?"

The words came racing at him. "The plane was delayed out of LaGuardia. Everything was fucked. I forgot to charge my cell phone. I stopped by to see Mom on my way over but she was asleep. I couldn't bear to wake her up. I sat with her for a while until they told me I had to leave. Now I'm too late to see Tommy. Shit."

"Where's Jacob?" Claudia asked.

Kim glanced over her shoulder, out into the darkness, as if she were also surprised by her husband's absence. "He couldn't make it today. Business. He's hoping to fly up tomorrow."

Nothing lasts with her, Scott thought. Nothing. "Well, you're here," he said. "Come sit down. Have some wine."

WHEN SCOTT WAS a child, his mother flirted and he watched. He slippered downstairs, swung around the banister's bottom column, and there she was. Men moved closer to her, reaching out to touch, blocking his way. His father always stood on the other side of the room.

Scott's father taught architecture at Penn; his mother helped with his projects, and they lived in Bryn Mawr. His mother liked to entertain, nearly every night. Neighbors, friends, visitors from out of town. "Party at the Fongs," they must have said, again and again. "See you at Walter and Isabel's."

On the first floor, Scott's father had replaced a few walls with elegant, polished oak beams, making what he called a "wide-open house." Loftlike. From the ceiling hung a narrow, dragon kite he'd carried back from his hometown of Linping, near Canton and the Pearl River delta. The kite ran across the top of the enormous room, corner to corner. Pink, white, red, green, and gold. Over the years the colors faded and the thin wood dried, until the dragon became as fragile as a blown bubble. It looked like an old, slow-winding snake, swaying amid the breathing and the smoke.

Smart men and women, well dressed, drinking, waved their cigarettes as they talked about new cities in distant lands, designs to improve the world and enrich the lives of every human being. Scott kept his head down. He focused on the people, their arms, legs, fingers, lips, and he guessed who would touch his mother next and where and for how long.

He kept track so he could tell Kim. He was ten and she was twelve. He always begged her to come downstairs with him.

"Scott," she'd say, "I'm uninterested in the foibles of their little world."

As children, they looked much more like each other than like their parents. Mixed faces, their father's small-boned frame, their mother's bumped nose. Straight black hair. The olive brown skin of European Jews. Nearsighted like their father, in glasses from kindergarten, but like their mother, they had brown eyes that opened wide. Even though Kim was two years older, when they were together, people took them for twins. She hated hearing it. He didn't.

She talked on the phone and studied and Scott had to go downstairs alone. When he returned, he brought her a cookie, brownie, or slice of pie, and for that she let him sit on her bed. Her room was nicer than his and he tried to spend as much time there as possible. It was on the third floor, so she could be by herself or together with her friends. The dormer windows gave her a view of the small Unitarian seminary across the street. Scott liked to stand close to the glass and watch people walk their dogs among the brick buildings. His room was on the second floor, catty-corner from his parents' bedroom. A maple tree blocked the view from his only window.

Their father had painted Kim's desk pink and she had a pink chair to match. She sat on it cross-legged, bending over her homework. Scott looked at the back of her neck, the knob of bone at the top of her spine.

"Kimmy," he said, "Mr. Shin kissed her on the lips. I counted to seven. Then Mr. Goodyall held her hand between his two hands and I counted to eighteen. Her face is red again, like a tomato. Her neck, too."

"I don't want to hear it. I'm busy with my math."

"Mr. Simone wanted to dance with her. His hands were on her hips. While he whispered to her, I saw him bite the bottom of her ear."

"Shh. I don't care. I don't even believe you."

"I'm not making it up. Come with me. I'll show you."

She turned around in her chair to face him. She rubbed her forehead with her palm. The gesture and the withering look made him feel dense and annoying. "I'll tell you something I've learned," she said. "The human body was made to be touched. It's what we're supposed to do. It's what we're designed for. That's why we have skin."

Scott looked at her cheeks, where her skin seemed dry. There were Braille bumps of red acne he could have tried to read with his fingertips. "Why does Dad stand so far from her, then?" he asked. "He doesn't touch her, or anyone else."

"Shut your mouth, Scott. Please. You need to grow up. Focus on the realities of our situation. You don't want to wind up like Dad." She turned back to her work.

During those early years, he often had no idea what his sister meant. But he wanted to stay in her room. That was one reality. He shut his mouth.

Soon after Kim arrived, Claudia went up to bed. "I'm sure you two could use some time together," she said.

Scott brought in another bottle and another glass. Kim stretched out on the couch, so he sat across from her in his reading chair. "Mom was anxious to see you," he said.

Kim shut her eyes and took a few deep breaths. "There's so much I need to tell her, Scott. I don't think I can handle it all."

"Jacob must be a comfort to you."

Before she said a word Scott could see the anger coming. She opened her eyes, sat up, and reached for her glass. "Oh," she said, "he doesn't understand. He comes home and tells me about what happened at the office, the projects he's pitching, as if I could get my mind off of this and onto that. I can hardly talk to him. He's too optimistic."

"Optimistic?"

"I'm not even sure he really knows me. It's hard for me to look him in the eye. He says she might have a year, not months. He keeps saying we might have time to have a baby for her."

"And?"

She sipped her wine and looked down at the floor. "Maybe I remarried too quickly," she said, her voice quieter.

"Are you two still working on getting pregnant?"

"We may not have to work on it anymore."

"What do you mean?"

She finished the wine in her glass and poured herself some more. Then she smoothed her blouse over her stomach. "It doesn't show? Good. It's almost two months. Jacob hasn't noticed yet either. I haven't told him. Don't you tell him. And don't tell Claudia, or Mom. I want to be the one to tell them."

AFTER HE GOT Kim settled and checked on Tommy, Scott climbed into bed and spooned himself beside Claudia. He couldn't sleep and he thought about Kim. A successful New York lawyer, thirty-seven now. Would pregnancy change her? And where was Jacob? Why hadn't she told him yet?

Kim was always running from one man directly into the arms of another. Like rungs on a ladder, the men were usually connected—friends, co-workers, tennis partners. But who knew where the ladder led? And what could be said of these men? They were more or less fine, convinced they were turning their lives around, certain they would last. Bruce the podiatrist, Franklin the urban planner, and currently at bat, Jacob the TV producer.

Each time, Kim talked about fate. She believed her heart left her no choice. She was powerless. She threw open her arms, slipped the rings on and off her finger.

Over the years, Scott had grown angrier with her. Kim

didn't offer justifications. She had no interest in couples therapy or therapy of any kind. She just wanted something more, or something different, and she took it. The men sometimes called Scott, stunned, seeking guidance, explanations. There was nothing he could tell them. He sounded to himself like a lame Buddhist. "It's not about you," he'd say. "Best to let it go."

His mother would call him, too, heartbroken. "Does she do this to me deliberately?" she'd ask. "Am I being punished?"

"I don't understand her either, Mom. She's your daughter. You should talk to her."

"Then she'll shut me out with the silent treatment. I can't take that again."

To Claudia, Scott would say, "You're a woman. Explain this to me."

She shrugged her shoulders. "I wish I could."

Sadly, Claudia knew something about fate and powerlessness. She was an only child who lost her parents before she turned twenty. Her marriage to Scott had been her second marriage. Seven years ago, she was pregnant, crazy in love, watching Daniel, her first husband, stretch for his daily jog. She stood at the front window of their Chestnut Hill duplex, her arms crossed on the small shelf of her belly, and she smiled as Daniel showed off how limber he was, high-stepping away down the sidewalk. Then, at the corner, he stumbled, collapsing from the aneurysm that killed him before she could get close enough to hear whatever last words he might have said. She knelt beside him on the cold concrete, beneath the full-leafed branches of an oak tree. He sighed up at her and was gone.

Claudia had told Scott about the day after Daniel's funeral.

She woke early and drove herself to the Planned Parenthood clinic where she peered through her windshield at the demonstrators and the poster-size photographs they carried. She told herself that one death deserved another. She asked herself if she'd be able to stop at two. For almost an hour she watched the pregnant women come and go. Then she drove back home.

SCOTT STOPPED TRYING to sleep when he heard footsteps on the stairs. He got up, pulled on sweatpants and a T-shirt, and walked down to the kitchen. Kim was there, in flannel pajamas and slippers, pacing. It took Scott a split second to realize she was talking on her cell phone.

"I'm so ready for you," she was saying. "I can't wait any longer."

When she saw Scott, she beckoned for him to come closer.

"Is that Jacob?" he asked.

She reached out and took his hand and held it to her neck while she spoke. His palm rested against her windpipe, his thumb stretched to the edge of her eczema.

"I can't stop talking to you," she said. "I need to see you."

Scott felt the words brush beneath his hand. He could hear bits of the voice coming through the receiver. *Baby, honey, bunny, pie.* Not Jacob's voice. That was clear. Her throat was warm and when she lifted his hand away, he could see the white of his fingerprints on her flushed skin. She held on to his hand and moved it to her chest, above her heart.

"I can't stop anything," she said. She looked into Scott's eyes. "This is how it feels."

He tried to pull his hand back, but she held on. "Kimmy," he whispered. "No."

"When?" asked the voice. "Tell me. Now? Are you alone?"

Scott tried to picture this new man's face.

"Alone," she said.

This is my sister, Scott thought. His stomach churned and knotted. Do something. What?

"I'll call you tomorrow," Kim said. "I've got to go." Then she hung up.

Scott sat at the kitchen table, arms crossed. How could she always surprise him with the same old thing? "Who is he, Kimmy?" he asked. "How are you doing this?"

Kim started to pace again, from the refrigerator, past the table, to the pantry door and back. "It's easy to criticize," she said, "but you're not in my situation."

"What is your situation this time? Is it his baby?"

"You can't understand. I don't want to settle for something. I don't want an ordinary life like this. Like yours."

"Let's not talk about me and my life right now. Whose baby is it?"

She pulled out a chair and sat across from him. "Jacob's," she said. "It's Jacob's and I'm going to have an abortion. That's one thing I've decided, Scott. Maybe you can't handle any more. Maybe I shouldn't have told you anything. Maybe you should just run along back to bed."

Scott didn't move. "What will we tell Mom?"

"Nothing. We won't tell her anything. I'll meet Jacob at the airport and I'll tell him it's over. Mom doesn't need to know."

"I can't believe this. You have to do this again? You have to do it now?"

"This is the first time, Scott. Now I know what it is to be completely in love. Maybe I want you to see."

"I've heard all this before. Bruce, Frank, and now it's Jacob's turn. What does he know? Does he know anything?"

"I don't want to hurt him. I'll tell him what he needs to know."

"Jesus," Scott said. He stood up, pulled a bottle of bourbon from a cabinet, poured himself a shot, and drank it down. He leaned back against the counter. He considered offering her a drink, but she was pregnant. Besides, she would take what she wanted. "What's so ordinary about my life?" he asked.

"Oh, Scott," she said. "I'm not saying anything's wrong with what you and Claudia have. I'm not judging anybody. It's like she's your pet and you're hers. Everything so unconditional and sweet. Where's the challenge in that?"

He had asked for it, but he didn't need her analysis. He shook his head, as if to keep her words out of his brain. "You're older than I am. You're supposed to know better. The challenge is to be good to each other, day after day. Honor. Cherish. Remember?"

"Sweet Scott, like I said. I want more. More than he's got to give. Look at Mom, right? Our mother, dying. We have one life and it's always leaving. I'm not going to make her mistake and get stuck with someone I only love a little."

"So you'll do what she wouldn't quite dare? Again? You're pregnant after trying for months. I don't understand, I—"

"I told you you couldn't understand. It's all right. Gideon and I promised not to worry about explaining ourselves to other people. We've wasted enough time trying to do that. People can choose to accept us or not."

"Some choice," he said.

"Choose, Scott," she said. "Choose, little brother. That's what you get to do."

Scott downed another shot of the bourbon and felt it burn. "The baby," he said. "Jacob wants that baby, and you're not even going to tell him about it, are you?"

"I'll tell him what he needs to know."

"Brr," Scott said, and he shivered. "So goddamn cold." He shook his head, thinking that he and Claudia wanted another child, that his mother wanted another grandchild, that Tommy would someday want a sibling. And then there was Jacob.

He felt sick and mean, but Kim looked excited about the future, confident. She crossed her legs and leaned back in her chair. He wanted to slap her with the hand she had gripped so tightly to her neck and chest. Instead, he pushed himself away from the counter and walked slowly upstairs.

IN BED AGAIN, naked, Scott stretched out on his back and stared through the dark at the ceiling. "I can't sleep," he said. "I can't fucking sleep."

Claudia turned to him. She kissed his forehead. She kissed his lips and sniffed the bourbon. "How much did you have?"

"Not enough," he said, pulling her to him.

She kissed his shoulder, reached a hand down to his thigh. "Was I dreaming," she said, "or did I hear someone say fucking?"

Sometimes when they made love they were so quiet that the silence seemed to Scott like another sensation, wrapped around them, bringing them closer, pressing them together. But he didn't want to be quiet, or sweet. Claudia was willowy and light, lithe like the dancer she once dreamed of becoming. Her legs were surprisingly strong. He rolled her over and pushed those legs up toward her chest. "Yes," he said, "let's fuck."

AFTERWARD, CLAUDIA RESTED her head on his chest and he straightened her hair with his fingers. "Our time is limited," she said. "We should do this every night."

"Do you think," he began, and then he stopped.

"What?"

"Do you think we're ordinary?"

"We live and we die," she said. "We fuck. We're all ordinary."

"I mean, do you think we gave up on something?"

Claudia rolled away from him, onto her back. "What was she saying to you down there?"

Weak light drifted into the room from a street lamp a half block away. It was just enough to gray the black shadows and transform the furniture—dressers, shelves, vanity—into dark, menacing shapes pressed up against the walls. "How often do you think of Daniel these days?" he asked.

"Scott," she said, "don't."

He knew about Claudia's nightmares. He knew about everything she couldn't help seeing in Tommy's beautiful face. All the possibilities of that other life. And here he was, in his worst moments, a replacement. The next-best thing. He sat up and shoved his pillow behind his back. "Sorry," he said. "She gets me going."

She sat up beside him. "What did she tell you?"

"Take a wild guess."

"She's cheating on Jacob, isn't she?"

"She's getting a divorce. And an abortion. And she hasn't told Jacob a thing."

Claudia sighed and crossed her arms at her stomach. "What does she expect you to do?"

"Nothing. She said I had to choose to accept her or not. She doesn't want me to tell anyone. Not Jacob. Not Mom. Not you."

"Poor Jacob," Claudia said.

Scott remembered the last time he'd seen Jacob, at that Boston wedding. They'd stood together by the bar late in the evening. The bar was busy and they glanced back at their wives. "I feel so lucky," Jacob said. "Your sister is my dream come true." Was there something Scott should have said in response? A gentle warning he could have offered? Some careful advice about the transience of luck and dreams? Perhaps, but he'd felt hopeful. He didn't want to jinx anything, so he'd kept silent. He'd wrapped his arm around Jacob's shoulders.

Now Scott put his arm around Claudia. "He was the best one yet," he said. "But she must think they'll keep getting better. She must think this new one is really perfect."

"He will be," Claudia said. "For a while. Then he'll be ordinary, too."

SCOTT AWOKE EARLY, hazed with a hangover. He had a few minutes before he needed to get everyone else up. Claudia slept soundly on her back beside him. He brushed her hair out of her eyes, ran his fingers down one of her arms, from her round shoulder to her thin knuckles. She shifted a leg, a smile came to her mouth, and she slept on.

He turned to check the clock and wound up looking at the row of framed photographs on his night table. He stared at his favorite image of his mother. She was irresistible in this picture, standing on the deck of a ship. Her dress and her snug pill-box hat are pink. Her neck seems longer than it is, and she's so young, a swan for swooning over. Audrey Hepburn, without the long gloves or the ebony cigarette holder. She's in profile, gazing off to shore, and there's fear in the set of her lips. She looks as if she's running away because she is. The sky above her is as heavy and gray as the steel deck beneath her white heels. Her parents don't know where she's bound. They don't even know she's leaving. A ticket for Italy is snapped shut in her black purse. Walter, her husband-to-be, waits for her. He's a Fulbright scholar in Rome, studying ruins. The sea wind lifts the wisps of dark hair above her eyes and ears. She's setting sail to get married.

One of Scott's theories was that flirting brought his mother closer to that younger, irresistible self. He'd seen it happen. Lips on her cheek, a hand in her hand, arms around her waist, and more color came, a blush, a glimmer to her eyes, the years washing away. It helped him to understand why his father might have stood on the other side of the room. He could watch the transformation from there, wait for her to cross the distance between them again.

THEY DROPPED TOMMY off with the neighbors and made it to the hospital just before seven. They could go into pre-op only one at a time. Scott hadn't decided what he would say and what he wouldn't say, so he hung back. Kim went in first and he sat with Claudia, sipping lousy coffee from a paper cup, watching the elevator doors open and close. "I have no idea what to do about my sister," Scott said. "Sometimes I don't know how I still love her."

"She's your sister," Claudia said. "You have to love her."

They waited in silence, holding hands until Kim returned. She stood in front of them and said, "Mom looks terrible."

"What did you tell her?" Scott asked.

"Ask her yourself. She's waiting for you."

He had to go two floors down and when he stepped out of the elevator, the place felt subterranean. The pre-op room was cavernous and cold, like a meat locker. The fluorescent bulbs seemed slightly off phase, flickering, making everything look as if it were about to go out.

A nurse led him to his mother, who was third in a line of seven gurneys. The nurse pulled a creamy white curtain behind her as she left, giving them what passed for privacy. He sat in a chair by his mother's side and took her hand. Her skin was pale and she looked like she hadn't slept any better than he had.

"Mom," he said. "How are you feeling?"

"I'm busy flirting with death, Scott," she said. "And let me tell you, he's quite a charmer."

"What did Kimmy tell you?"

"Oh, nothing new. She's getting another divorce. She wanted me to know it was my fault. Apparently I taught her not to settle for a loveless marriage."

"That's not true, Mom."

"Well," she said, "I agree. But I did flirt. She's right about that."

Scott hated seeing her like this. Even in such a sterile place he thought he could smell death coming. Surgery and chemo and drugs wouldn't stop it this time. "Mom," he said, "we can talk about whatever you want."

"There *were* times I was tempted, but we're always tempted. As long as we're alive."

"Who was the most tempting?"

"What kind of question is that?" she said. She was smiling, though, so he kept going.

"Tell me, Mom. And tell me why."

"Well, there was that gardener we hired to do the hedges. He had cute little dimples."

"Really?"

"No. He had those dimples, but he was a moron. Nothing like Jules, who once dated that Broadway broad. I did enjoy the way he wanted me. His French accent. 'Just give me a weekend in Provincetown,' he would say. 'I will change your life.'"

"Who else?"

"Howard was so goddamn funny. He'd wink at me and I'd be laughing. And then there was Alvin, from Hong Kong. His hands were lovely. He made me a birthday vase every year with those hands. It was almost more than I could stand."

"How did you stop yourself?"

"You make it sound miraculous. Is it so hard to believe?"

"Not for me. But maybe for Kimmy."

She tried to sit up. "Help me adjust this damn bed," she said. He fiddled with it and got it to incline. She was looking better already. She went on. "I loved your father. That's all. That was always the fact. Everything else was simply idle speculation."

Was she just revising her past, or was she telling him the truth? It was what he wanted to believe about her and he decided to believe it.

She must have sensed his hesitation. "I never remarried, did I?" she asked.

He shook his head. He could hear a gurney being pushed out of the room, the wheels squeaking across the floor, voices saying, "You'll be all right, you'll be all right." He knew he should leave time for Claudia, but he had more to say now that they'd started. "Your flirting used to make me so angry," he said. "Once Dad and I went outside about it."

"What happened?"

"It was in the middle of a party. I was fifteen. We walked out to the driveway. I asked why he let you flirt and drink, night after night. I told him it made me sick. I shouted at him."

"Oh, Scott. What did he say?"

"He made me wait. It was late summer, a little chilly, and he looked so thin. He had that black leather belt that wrapped almost twice around his waist. He sighed and shoved his hands deep into his pockets, like he did. 'I accept her,' he said."

She laughed and it sounded to him like one of her old laughs. It echoed around them. "What did you do then?"

"I shouted some more until he said, 'It's who she is. It doesn't lead to anything.'"

"And then?"

"That's all I remember," Scott said. "Maybe we hugged," he added, even though he had a clear picture in his mind of how he'd turned away, shocked at the tears in his eyes, walking toward the street, past the line of cars. Music and clatter washed out of the house. After a few steps, he'd called out above the noise, loud enough for his father and others to hear: "It does lead to something, Dad!"

He sat there in silence for a moment, trying to hold on to his mother's laugh, the burst and joy of it.

"Tell me," she said. "You and Claudia are doing all right together, aren't you?"

"We're doing well, Mom. I love her like crazy."

His mother reached for his wrist and looked at his watch. "Go on," she said. "I'll be fine. Tell Claudia to hurry down here."

THE SURGERY TOOK HOURS, as they knew it would. Just after three o'clock, the surgeon came out to tell them that the tumor was larger than expected. He couldn't say for certain if he'd managed to get it all out.

A little later, they were allowed to see her again, still one at a time, and only for a few minutes each. Kim had walked away to make a phone call, so Scott went in first. His mother was upstairs now, on the fourth floor, in a room with a window, but she had looked much better underground. An IV was threaded into her wrist and another tube was sticking into her side. Several different nurses buzzed in and out of the room. "Your mother's on Dilaudid," one of them said. "She probably won't remember much of what she says, let alone what you say."

Scott could barely look at her. He thought the tumor must have weighed forty or fifty pounds. She seemed that much lighter. A waif beneath a sheet, too frail to ever move again.

It was clearly work for her to turn to face him, but she did. "I'd like to see Tommy," she whispered.

"I'll bring him by first thing tomorrow."

"I'd like to see Walter, too. But that won't be tomorrow, will it?"

"That won't be for a long time, Mom."

"Poor Kimmy. She's more like me than I am."

"That doesn't make sense, Mom."

She shut her eyes. "It will," she said.

THEY HAD TWO CARS with them at the hospital since Kim wanted to be able to meet Jacob at the airport. As they were getting ready to leave, she asked Scott to drive with her. "I was talking to Jacob on the phone," she said. "He wanted me to bring you along."

Scott looked at Claudia. She shrugged her shoulders. "I'll pick up Tommy and meet you at home," she said.

He hugged her. "We'll be there soon," he told her, but he didn't know what he meant by *we*. He hoped that his mother had somehow changed Kim's mind. How could he possibly hope that? He had seen and heard too much. But hope he did. Maybe she would relent. Maybe she would at least take more time to think it over.

She drove him away from the hospital. Freezing rain was pouring down. When they merged onto Route 76, Kim said, "Jacob's not flying in. I want you to come with me to the clinic. I made an appointment yesterday. That's one reason I was late."

Scott no longer knew what to say or do. "What did you tell Jacob?"

"I told him Mom's illness was making me think about a lot of things. I told him I needed some time and space."

"That's a nice use of Mom."

"Just help me through this, Scott," she said. "Please."

"Did you bring me along to make me feel terrible or because you need me?"

She looked away from the road, over at him, for so long it made him nervous. "Can it be both?" she said.

WEEKS LATER, NEAR the end of January and another round of chemo, Scott's mother set out for an afternoon walk to the library, returning books, carrying in her pocket a list of new ones she hoped to find on the shelves. It was an unseasonably warm day. She had one of her old scarves wrapped around her head. Rushing to cross Lancaster Avenue in front of a speeding car, she suffered a massive heart attack.

Scott wondered if she hadn't run out into traffic in search of a quicker ending. He could have understood that. It hadn't been possible for her to be an extraordinary patient this time. She was scared to eat because digesting was so painful. The drugs never seemed to do the right thing. She would only see Tommy for five minutes at a time and even those brief visits exhausted her.

Scott hoped she hadn't been afraid when it happened. He cried with Claudia, wishing he could have done something better for his mother, something better than sitting with her and keeping her company and doing whatever she asked.

Kim came in for the funeral with her new man. The day was full of bluster and cold. The funeral parlor had covered the area around the grave with bright green artificial turf so no one would have to stand in mud and slush. It was a cross-cultural ceremony. They burned paper money. They tore strips of black cloth. They left food and firecrackers at the headstone that now had two names carved into it. The new man held Kim close and she sobbed louder than anyone.

But Scott knew none of that as Kim drove him toward the clinic. She made one wrong turn and he didn't correct her. It slowed them down, but she figured it out and found her way to the building she wanted.

Scott said nothing. It was getting dark and the rain banged against the windshield. It was too ugly outside for demonstrators.

"Trust me," she said. "It's for the best."

"I can't believe I'm here in this place with you."

"I want to be able to give him everything. We'll have everything, right from the beginning. You'll see."

Scott thought of his mother, in the hospital, her hand wrapped around his wrist as she looked at his watch. He thought of Claudia, years ago, parked in front of a clinic like this one. He could almost see her out on the sidewalk, kneeling over her first husband, feeling his skin, amazed and frightened at how quickly it grew cold.

"Kimmy," he said, "it doesn't work that way. We don't get everything."

She unbuckled her seat belt, leaned across, and kissed his cheek. "You don't," she said.

What to Expect

I. Before Becoming Pregnant

When Claude Martin was younger, he owned a forest green MGB. He called that car a death trap and he treasured it. After he dropped the top, he'd pull on Italian leather gloves, snap them tight at his wrists. Then he'd rev the engine. Listen to it purr.

The steering thrilled him, but it terrified his passengers, especially Ellen Farrell. Her first time in the car, he kept reassuring her as they cruised north from Philadelphia to picnic in New Hope. The narrow road snaked along the banks of the Delaware River. It was a warm, early June Saturday and Claude sported buzz-cut black hair, gold-framed aviator sunglasses, khakis, a burgundy polo shirt. He explained the design of the car. "It's fluid," he said. He lifted a hand from the wheel and flapped his fingers like a rudder, trying to illustrate what he was saying about the tie-rods and the gears: "It slips from tense to slack. You have to adjust constantly. You need nerve."

To clarify, he accelerated into a turn. "Don't worry," he said. "I have everything under control." The MG flirted with a fishtail, sliding toward the shimmering water. Ellen screamed. Then the car caught, kept its line, growled around the bend. "Hold on!" Claude shouted, the river wind blasting past them.

This was 1974. Claude was twenty-three, smack in the middle of his heyday, and he was wooing Ellen hard. She had on a sky blue sundress, a cloud white cardigan, and sandals soled with worn Pirellis. "Heavenly," Claude would say. He walked through town by her side, watching her admire the redbrick houses, the antiques that filled the stores. Something about the quaintness of the place, or the shine of her blonde hair, made him think of high school marching band, how he lugged the French horn and lusted after the majorette. When Ellen wasn't looking, Claude bought her a wooden whirligig. He hid it in the picnic basket until they were on the edge of town, close to the river, sitting on a blanket in the grass. They could see a half-dozen fishermen in waders, casting quietly for shad.

The whirligig was a rainbow-colored propeller atop a short spindle and Claude knelt to present it. "Let's see it fly," Ellen said, so he stood and spun it into the air. It shot straight up above them, then floated over the river, settling onto the surface of the brown water like a bright bug. The fishermen were not about to waste time rescuing a whirligig. Claude went out after it, shoes and socks off, his khakis rolled up to his knees. When he slipped and fell, splashing down face first, the fishermen scowled and Ellen cracked up. He looked back at her, surprised that her laughter sounded so similar to her screaming, full bodied and rich, a high note hit right.

Soaked, he sat shirtless in the sun, drying, as he told Ellen how, despite the unfortunate crash of the whirligig, he dreamed of becoming an air force pilot. "I have the perfect build for it," he said, and anyone could see he spoke the truth. Thick, quick arms and a low center of gravity ready to handle supersonic speeds. A strong compact body designed for cockpits and flight suits. He looked across the river at New Jersey and talked about the missions he would fly. "F-4s and U-2s. All over the world," he said. "It's too bad I'm antiwar."

Instead of ascending the ranks, he planned to be a commercial pilot, or maybe he would make money in sales and buy beachfront property until he commanded a real-estate empire.

Ellen folded her cardigan into a pillow and stretched out on her back. "Do you want a big family?"

Claude turned to her. He hadn't given a great deal of thought to children. What would he do with children? "A big family," he said, testing the sound of it. "You mean kids?"

She smiled. "Yes," she said. "Little people. Like you, only smaller. Then larger."

He leaned over her. Before they kissed, he said, "One step at a time."

AFTER THAT, THEY had three years together. Three years of laughter, step by step and side by side. Wedding, honeymoon, baby boy. They named their son Larry. He started small and kept growing, and they kept driving that MG out of the city, into the countryside, where it was easier to dream through their weekends and holidays. They wanted to have another child and soon they were ready to start trying again, but Ellen came down with a sore throat, which turned out to be cancer, and it carried her away, leaving Claude alone with their two-year-old boy.

You have to adjust constantly, Claude told himself, but he could not adjust. You need nerve, he knew, but his was gone. At the funeral, by the grave, holding his son in his arms, Claude said, again and again, "I may not be sturdy enough for this."

He did not intend to be a man who couldn't recover, but as time passed, what he drove and what he dreamed changed, down to the white Taurus taxi of his early fifties. He never became a pilot of any kind. He never bought land and he never bought a house. Instead, he picked up strangers, took them where they wanted to go, gathered in their fares and tips.

CLAUDE COULD HEAR Ellen whisper through the sing-song of Larry's voice. The boy had his mother's hazel eyes and, early on, Claude made plans for keeping her memory alive in Larry's mind. He prepared himself for the questions long before they came: Where is she? What was she like? Is she coming back? Claude wasn't overly mystical; he tried not to spook Larry, didn't say a word about ghosts. Instead, he mentioned her favorite dress, how well she could throw a baseball, the warmth of her skin, how her neck blushed light pink when she was upset or pleased. He made a photograph album. He tried to be concrete. Still, when they were outside, alone, walking through their northeast Philly neighborhood or just sitting on the stoop, Claude would sometimes point up at the sky. "That's where she might be right now," he'd say. "Looking down and watching over. Proud of you."

Claude did his best and he surprised himself for a while, until he started drinking more. He stayed out later, let Larry spend the nights with cousins and friends. He tried a few sales jobs—insurance, siding, cutlery—before trading in the MG for a taxi. During his first week as a cabby he decided he wasn't a good father, he accepted it as fact, and he waited for the punishment to come down on him.

Against all odds, Larry grew up kind, good natured, and sharp. There were so many ways for a kid to go wrong, and yet Larry was a hardworking student with an aptitude for engineering. They had some great days together—Phillies games at Veterans Stadium, the planetarium at the Franklin Institute, cheesesteaks at Jim's, milkshakes at the Country Club Diner. Still, what difference could such moments make? Most days were not great at all. Claude looked for resentment in his son's hazel eyes; he looked for disappointment, but he saw only love and adoration he felt he did not deserve.

He allowed himself to believe that Larry was a gift given to him by Ellen. Maybe two years with her had been enough to mold him irrevocably into a good child, beyond the reach of a father's bad behavior. Two years in Ellen's hands could change a whole life, Claude knew that much. When Larry was awarded a scholarship by Dickinson College, in central Pennsylvania, Claude felt that he and his son had somehow turned a corner.

. . .

A WEEK BEFORE Larry went away, Claude bought a six-year-old Malibu—vinyl topped and tan. He used it to take Larry up to college. He also used it to visit, and during those first two months, he visited often. Weekend after weekend he drove back and forth on the turnpike, four hours round-trip, to take Larry out for a meal. He'd leave early in the morning. The Malibu could roar past the trucks that ran open throttle down the Blue Mountains. Near the Susquehanna River, he almost always hit fog. The trucks switched on their flashers and blew their air horns. Claude liked stopping at an exit outside Shepherdstown to call, just to say he was closing in. The road went uphill for a while from there and he rose above the fog. Then he rolled on through it again, down to his son's door.

They often took drives before they ate. If Larry had time, they'd spend the day in the car. They went south to Gettysburg. They wound along the Susquehanna, up into the Appalachians. The whole state was greener than Claude expected. They sped to Pittsburgh. Altoona, Johnstown, Latrobe, Mount Pleasant. He loved how the Malibu hugged the road. Even more, he loved glancing across at Larry. His son was an inch short of six feet, thin like a track star, a long-limbed hurdler. Claude had to stop himself from being annoying. How did you come out so good? he wanted to ask. How do you keep getting better?

One weekend when the leaves had begun to turn, they stopped at a vista point to watch the colors come. They sat on the warm hood and tapped the backs of their shoes against the bumper as they looked out. In the valleys, people were mining coal, forging steel, pressing paper. It was the sixth weekend in a row Claude had visited.

"Dad," Larry said, "I'm getting pretty busy with schoolwork."

"I'm sure you are, son. Dickinson is a serious place. Makes me proud to see you here."

"Midterms are coming up. I'm worried about falling behind."

"Don't worry. I'm driving back tonight. We'll grab an early dinner and then I'm on the road."

"I need more time to work, Dad. It's great that you keep driving all the way—"

Claude put a hand on Larry's shoulder, not wanting to hear the *but* and what would come after. He saw plumes of smoke above the low mountains, twisting up into the sky like ropes, attached to nothing. "Say no more, son. From now on, you want a visitor, you let me know. Otherwise, I'll wait for the vacations, like everyone else."

A FEW WEEKS LATER, Claude felt the urge to make a spontaneous visit, but he decided to call first. It was early on a Saturday morning and he was driving downtown, toward the art museum, along the Schuykill River. A sculler practiced on the water. Claude pulled over to watch, listening for the splash of the oars. He imagined sculling sometime, but he would go in the middle of the day, the boathouses bright in the light, the sun beating down on his back. He wondered if Dickinson had a crew team. Then he was looking for a pay phone.

"Hello," Larry said.

Claude could tell right away his son had been sleeping. "Sorry to wake you. It's me."

"Dad? It's not even six yet. Is everything okay?"

"I thought I might come up for a visit."

"When?"

"I could leave in a few minutes, get there in time for breakfast."

"This is pretty sudden."

"I'd like to see you. Plus I feel like driving. There's a gorgeous day brewing."

"It's really a crazy busy time for me, Dad."

Claude coughed. Then he said, "Got it. Loud and clear. Maybe another time."

"Yeah, another time would be better."

As he drove out on Route 76, Claude considered making the trip anyhow. Even if he couldn't see Larry, it would be a pleasure to see the campus, take a walk, learn more about the college. Besides, if he was actually there, at the door, he felt certain Larry would find time to visit. Just before he reached the tollbooth, though, he wasn't sure. So he turned around.

CLAUDE STAYED AWAY from Dickinson, figuring his overdue punishment had begun. But after graduation, Larry moved home for a few years, and they were back to sharing the northeast Philly apartment. They seemed to get along fine. Larry became an independent contractor, a well-educated fix-up man. Claude kept his cab loaded with advertisements for his son, attracting several clients that way. It was a nice arrangement while it lasted. They drank together every now and then, even talked of saving up to invest in a house. Larry could renovate it and they could begin making some bigger money.

Then Larry found Jennifer.

II. How Your Appearance May Change

Larry was twenty-four when he met Jennifer Hollins at a Dickinson alumni party one summer night, downtown in a decaying apartment where the tenants had worked hard to brighten a dreary space. Larry stayed in the kitchen. Large images of baked goods hung from the walls. He liked his spot near the keg, beneath a painting of an enormous blueberry cupcake. Jennifer walked over for a refill and he pumped while she poured. He thought her hair was the color of a pink grapefruit. Her lips were the same color. As he studied the cupcake canvas with her, he speculated about the flavor of the glaze, the number of eggs required, the freshness of the berries, until Jennifer said, "Quit sweet-talking me."

She followed him out onto the fire escape, where they discussed life after Dickinson. "I'm an independent contractor," he said. "A handyman."

"I work in the development office at UPenn," she said. "But this summer I'm at Temple, attending a seminar on how to grow endowments."

Larry tried to guess which side of thirty she was on. He kept quiet.

"It sounds kinkier than it is," she said.

They looked down at the alley, across at a brick wall, skyward into the city's haze of lights and smoke. Above them glimmered a thin slice of moon, an off-kilter smile shining through the muck. Larry heard Jennifer inhale before she kissed his cheek. A little peck. The chasteness of it put her in her twenties, he thought. Then it was just her lips, and age left his mind.

He had his hands in her hair and on her back when she stopped him. She stepped away. "I'm too old for you," she said.

"No, you're not," Larry said. It seemed like a childish thing to say, so he added, "You don't feel too old. You don't look too old."

She moved closer again and placed her fingers gently over his lips. "Shut up," she whispered.

LARRY STOPPED SLEEPING at home. He stayed with Jennifer in her Manayunk house and he had no desire to be anywhere else. It was a feeling he didn't want to risk describing, so he kept it to himself. He tried to worry about the age difference. He did the math. She was thirty. When she was forty, he'd be thirty-four. When he was fifty, she would already have been fifty for years. The way he saw it, they'd have a better chance of dying together. They'd be less likely to leave each other alone.

One night, before dinner, his father caught him packing up a box of clothes and toiletries. "What is it with this woman?" Claude asked.

"You'll like her," was all Larry would say.

Another night, Claude asked about her age. "She's that much older?" he said. "Marrying young and early makes sense to me. After all, our time is limited. But marrying someone so much older, that I don't understand."

"Who said anything about marriage?" Larry asked.

Then, after Larry had been with Jennifer for three months, he told his father it was time to talk.

"I'm going to like her, right?" Claude asked.

"You"d better."

"Why?"

"Two reasons."

"Let's hear 'em."

"Well, we're getting married."

"And?"

"And," Larry said, "we're pregnant."

FATHERS ARE ALSO EXPECTANT, Larry read some-where. He added a corollary: But not nearly as expectant as grandfathers. Claude began dropping by Manayunk with books and videos. He'd pull up in the Taurus and take the concrete steps two at a time, like a schoolboy home at last. When Larry opened the door, his father would be standing there with the newest material tucked under his arm. "A pregnant fare rec-ommended this," he'd say. Or "I heard about this on the ra-dio." But, really, he just wanted to touch the baby-to-be. He'd put the latest stuff down and reach out for Jennifer's belly. He reached out with both hands.

Larry watched it happen again and again, like a ritual. Jennifer would practice the relaxation technique she was learn-ing. She took deeper breaths. She straightened her spine. He knew she was imagining a string lightly tugging up on the center of her head. She counted slowly or whispered the word *peace* to herself as she smiled and moved closer to Claude. "Grandpa's here," she said to their growing child. "Give him a kick."

"Oh," Claude would say. "*Bam!* I sure felt that."

• • •

Larry and Jennifer had their own more private ritual. Once a month with an old Polaroid. It was Jennifer's idea. It struck Larry as risky, something like a jinx. What would they do with the photographs if there was a miscarriage? But he didn't argue. When they got home on the chosen Friday, they hurried to the bedroom. They stripped off their clothes. Jennifer started in the doorway, standing with her back straight against the frame. She wanted him to construct a complete photo record and he tried to capture her breasts growing heavier, closer to her rounding belly, her skin there and there lining lightly with blue. He focused on the puffiness of her joints, the downy new hair swirling at the corners of her jaw.

The books said sex was okay if it felt okay. The seal was airtight. The baby was in the bag, so to speak. It could even find the rhythm soothing. Larry wanted his future child to recognize his voice from the very start. He sang to it instead of moaning Jennifer's name: *Oh baby baby baby*.

III. Dreams and Nightmares

Jennifer had performed the pregnancy test in the bathroom. Her eyes had been on the two small circles and the pink lines that appeared, first one and then the other. It took her a moment to notice that Larry had dropped to one knee on the tile floor. He opened his hand. A penny-size pink rubber band sat on his palm. "We talked about doing this someday," he said. "Today is someday."

Jennifer took the rubber band from him and held it up to get a closer look. "How romantic," she said. "And what a beautiful Philadelphia diamond."

"Marry me," he said.

"These tests can be wrong, you know."

"Marry me, Jennifer."

She tried to picture him as her husband. She tried to see him as a father. She wanted an image, a fantasy of the future to float through her mind. What would he look like in his thirties? Would he become a drinker? Would her parents, may they rest in peace, have approved? Would he roughhouse the baby too much? Would his ears get hairy? Nothing came to her. She closed her eyes and opened them and she could see only what was in front of her. He was kneeling at her feet. She was standing there, looking down, loving him like crazy.

"Ask me once more," she said, slipping the rubber band around her ring finger.

EVERYONE SHE KNEW seemed to have a delivery tale to tell. Again and again, people wanted her to hear how birth could be given anywhere. Just like that. There's no knowing, they said. In these stories, there was desperation and panic, leading up to a critical moment. Then kind strangers appeared from nowhere, bringing with them one happy ending after another. A paramedic calmly issued instructions over a cell phone. The cops switched on their sirens to serve as escorts. The mousy woman eating alone by the door turned out to be an off-duty obstetrician.

Still, she couldn't stop thinking about the many problems

that could develop all at once or little by little. Her friends kept the bad stories to themselves, but the books held nothing back. Even in her favorite guide, the longest chapter was called "When Something Goes Wrong" and it began with a warning: "This chapter should be read only by those women who have a suspected or diagnosed complication; and even then reading should be confined to the problem at issue. Casual reading could lead to not-so-casual, and unnecessary, worrying."

She tried to skip those pages, but she couldn't. She read every one.

HER MOST PERSISTENT nightmare started the night Claude brought over the first book. It was after eleven and he'd probably been drinking. He slouched into a kitchen chair, leaned on the table, and began by complaining about his cab. "Cars have become so simple," he said. "Automatic boxes. Just point and go. No wonder people fall asleep at the wheel. Fortunately, I have developed a system to combat boredom."

"Vodka?" Larry asked.

"It has to do with bursts of speed, son. I'll say no more." He slid the book across the table. "Here," he said.

Larry paged through it, pausing occasionally to take a closer look at the drawings and charts. "Daunting," he said. On the front cover, a peaceful pregnant woman sat calmly in a wooden rocker, reading. On the back, a happy, diapered baby crawled toward a bright garden.

"I'll tell you the kind of book I want," Claude said. "There could be a whole series of them: *What to Expect when You're*

Exhausted, What to Expect when You're Expiring, What to Expect when You Have No Expectations."

"Dad," Larry said. "Let's be more festive here. What do you think it's important for us to know at this point?"

"Read the book," he said.

Jennifer put on a pot of coffee. She believed it was good for Claude to talk about the past. Speech over silence, even if she sometimes kept herself quiet. "Tell us what you remember," she said. "Please."

"You would have liked Ellen," he said. "If she were here, she'd tell you plenty. She'd tell you all about it."

"I wish I could have met her," said Jennifer. She watched Larry walk over to massage his father's tense shoulders. He was careful, using a lighter touch than he used with her. Claude's bones looked so close to his skin. She smiled when Larry stayed with his questioning: "Come on, Dad. What was Mom like when she was pregnant?"

Claude rubbed his eyes with his palms and spoke slowly. "Everything was different then," he began. "And she was younger. Twenty-two. I worked and she handled all the arrangements. But I can tell you about the delivery."

"Tell us," Jennifer said.

"At first, I was watching through a little round window in the door and I couldn't see a thing. But one of the nurses was a friend of ours. She got me in scrubs, took me inside, and told me where to stand. Your mother was screaming. I'd heard her scream before, but never like that. Like the whistle from a steam engine, bearing down. Inhuman. It went on and on.

There wasn't room for me to move closer to her, so I just stood there, listening. Eventually, they decided to do a Cesarean. I turned away. Then I turned back. I couldn't believe how much fluid there was. I watched it splash against the floor. Then I heard screaming again, but it was you this time, and they were lifting you up."

"Cesarean," Jennifer said, and the thought scared her, but then she was trying to imagine Larry as a newborn and it shocked her how easy it was to do. Though she couldn't imagine him older, it took less than a second to see him in a baby's body, splotchy pink, squinty eyed, baggy skinned, his hair plastered to his soft head, his chubby arms waving in the air, someone holding him aloft. It was just as easy to imagine Claude as a baby. She saw the two of them side by side, banging their tiny fists against the table.

That was how the nightmare began. In the weeks that followed, Jennifer would fall asleep and find herself facing the baby twins in various locations—the bathroom, her office, her bed, the supermarket. They liked to take her by surprise. They crawled under the stall door, climbed out of a file cabinet, made fish faces at her from behind the deli counter. They had many adorable outfits. She, however, stayed stubbornly the same. She didn't get any younger. Baby Claude and baby Larry were unrelenting, crying and crying until she was so angry that she screamed. No one anywhere heard her. The crying drowned her out.

Still, she poured coffee for Claude each time he came over. "Stay the night," she'd say. "We've got plenty of room. You've done enough driving."

IV. Labor

During the third trimester, Larry started working for Kazuo Shiroyama, a forty-eight-year-old recent immigrant who'd decided to make money in martial arts education. He wanted his row house basement converted into a karate studio and he hired Larry to paint, put in mats and mirrors, build a changing cubicle, install a folding partition. There was duct work, rewiring, and plumbing. Larry drew up plans and followed them step by step.

Shiroyama had his office in his sunroom, right off the kitchen. It had tatami floors and a heavy bag. On his first morning of work, Larry found Shiroyama out there pummeling that bag. Those hands can kill, Larry thought. Shiroyama was barefoot, in blue jeans and a white V-neck T-shirt, his fists and feet smashing into the bag. There were no chairs in the room, just two low tables. One was a desk, clutter-free, except for a thermos and two Japanese teacups. The other table held a VCR and a TV. An image from a karate tournament was paused on the large color screen.

When Larry walked in, Shiroyama stopped his workout. He waved Larry over. "Show what you can do," he said.

Larry raised his fists and hunched like a boxer. He jabbed the bag. It didn't move much.

Shiroyama used his index finger to push up Larry's chin. "No hunching," he said. "Keep your head back. Away from enemy. Now snap your wrist. Rotate your fist as you hit. Like a corkscrew. This adds torque to the punch." He demonstrated a slow-motion right jab. His forearm had the veins of a horse leg.

Larry hit the bag twice more. It hurt his hand.

"Better," Shiroyama said. "Do ten rights and ten lefts. Take your time. Concentrate."

Shiroyama picked up a black cotton sweater and put it on while Larry jabbed. "I was once a student of Master Ohkawa," Shiroyama said. "Master Ohkawa shaved his head and went into the Shikoku wilderness alone. He punched and kicked tree trunks. His feet sharpened into ax blades. His fists became sledgehammers. His skin grew tougher than bark. I want to make my students powerful like that." He adjusted his sweater. Then he sat on the floor and rested his arms on his table. "Let's drink," he said, pouring out two cups of green tea.

Larry sat across from him. He nodded toward the paused image on the screen. "What were you watching?" he asked.

"Fukuoka, 1986," Shiroyama said. "I was foolish." He flicked the remote and the tape advanced.

Whoever shot the video must have stood off at a distance, without a zoom lens. But Larry could see Shiroyama, a black belt around his waist, wailing away on a tall guy, pounding out a quick rhythm. Jab, jab, uppercut, kick. Kick, kick, jab. They were fighting in something like a boxing ring, except it was larger than that, and there were no ropes, just other people sitting around the edges of the mats, cross-legged and cheering. The tall guy wobbled.

"Here I thought the round was over," Shiroyama said, pointing a finger at the TV.

Larry watched as the younger Shiroyama dropped his hands for a moment. The tall guy leapt at the opening. He straightened up and roundhoused his foot into Shiroyama's temple. Shiroyama seemed to bow right into the blow. It knocked him flat.

"Ouch," Larry said.

Shiroyama smiled. "Yes," he said. He switched the set off. "If I had won that fight, who can say? But when you let your guard down, your head is kicked."

Larry sat on the tatami with his hands around his teacup. "Can I ask you a question?"

"Yes," said Shiroyama. "Then to work."

"Do you have any children?"

"Why do you ask that?"

"Thinking about things I didn't see coming," Larry said. "Plus I'm asking everyone these days."

Shiroyama inhaled. He sipped his tea. Then he twisted his thick fingers together. "I have been married," he said. "Before I moved to America, my wife took me to Hokkaido. She knew I liked exotic foods, not available here. We ate bear, sea lion, blowfish, and whale. I thought the bear tasted best. My wife didn't enjoy any of them. She said there was too much muscle."

Larry waited for more, but Shiroyama just stared out the windows, toward the row houses across the street. "So," Larry said, "no children?"

Shiroyama untwisted his hands and looked at them closely, as if he hoped to find a baby hidden in his palms. "No," he said. "No children."

• • •

V. Further Preparations

Jennifer found something charming in Claude's extensive preparations, but they were not entirely comforting. He told her he always kept an eye out for pregnant women who needed a ride because he wanted to practice, and he liked to show her how well stocked he kept his cab—his "maternity ward on wheels." Half of his trunk was filled with resealable plastic bags that held skin lotion, baby powder, sugarless candy, polar fleece socks, a set of washcloths, granola bars, a box of raisins. There was a blanket, a gallon of spring water, a deck of cards, a box of diapers, a stack of magazines, a baby-naming book the size of an amulet.

One night, when Larry was late coming home from Shiroyama's, Claude stopped by, more excited than usual. Jennifer let him feel her belly for a kick. She used the moment to check his breath for alcohol. She smelled coffee, sweat, and sleeplessness. He pulled a stopwatch from his pocket. "Before I came over here," he said, "I timed a few runs to the hospital. It was a slow night, so I tried a few different routes. I swear I could be an ambulance driver. You want to see how fast we can get there from here?"

"I don't think so."

Claude clicked the stopwatch on and off. "Is Larry still at the karate-man's?" he asked.

"Yes."

"He's spending a lot of time there, isn't he? Can you explain that to me?"

"There's a lot I can't explain," Jennifer said. She was tempted to go on: I can't explain why you don't get your own life. Or why I tolerate your trembling hands. Nothing could be easy for Claude, she knew. He was reaching out, wanting only to be part of the family. She wanted to be able to trust him. Larry liked to say that the pregnancy was making Claude more hopeful, better than he'd been in years. Maybe that was true. But maybe it was making him more unstable.

She inhaled. Exhaled. "Can I get you some coffee or anything?"

VI. Choosing the Right Exercise when Pregnant

During lunch breaks, Shiroyama occasionally gave Larry lessons. One day, Larry was walking outside to his truck when Shiroyama waved him into the sunroom office. The VCR was running again. Larry didn't think this tape had anything to do with the martial arts, unless it was a documentary about Master Ohkawa's wilderness. The trees on the screen did not appear threatening—they were thin trunked, short, bent like old rice farmers, surrounded by raked silver sand. It would have been cruel to disturb them with kicks and punches. There were three small gray boulders in a line. A woman's voice talked high and sweet as the camera moved. Larry didn't understand a word she was saying.

Shiroyama held the remote in his hand, but he let the tape play on for a few minutes. When the camera panned over to a red wooden gate, he switched it off.

Larry noticed a slight hunch to Shiroyama's back. "Japan?" he asked. "Your wife talking?"

"Yes," Shiroyama said, standing straighter. "Correct." Then

he set the remote down and picked up a pair of pads, a small version of the leg pads worn by hockey goalies. He strapped them to his forearms, held them at chest level, and told Larry to swing away. After the first two punches Shiroyama shouted, "Come on! This is not tai chi! This is karate school!"

Larry kept swinging. "*Yoisha!*" he shouted, as he had been taught.

"Better. More with the left. And breathe."

"*Yoisha!*"

Shiroyama seemed to glide around the room as Larry lumbered after him, punching at the pads, until Shiroyama said, "Stop. Good. You are becoming stronger. I may need your help with advertising. It will involve an outdoor practice, something for people to see. Will that be all right?"

"Sure," said Larry.

That Friday, Jennifer picked up the Polaroid herself. "You get naked first this time," she told Larry.

He obeyed.

She directed him to the doorway. "Okay, now pretend you're pregnant."

He filled his belly with air. He tried to expand.

"Pretend you're holding the baby," she said.

"Toss me a pillow."

"No props," she said.

Larry didn't know what to do with his hands. He imagined one holding the baby's head, another holding the back. He spread his fingers wide. The flash popped. Jennifer pulled out the developing picture and tossed it onto the comforter. She aimed at him again.

"The baby's crying," she said.

"No, it's not," said Larry. He moved his hands closer to his body. He thought of what he'd seen other fathers do. "I'm bouncing the baby now," he said. "Did you hear that? It just burped." Larry grinned and made a funny noise with his lips. He moved his hands up to his shoulders. "Now I'm giving it a piggyback ride."

"You have no idea how small the baby will be," Jennifer said, setting the camera on her night table.

Larry stepped over to her and reached for her blouse, but she stopped his hand. She lifted it away from her buttons and then she took his other hand, too. "What are you doing to yourself?" she asked. "They're even worse today."

The knuckles of his index and forefingers were scabbed, swollen, bruised dull brown and purple. "Sledgehammers," he said. "Shiroyama says I'm getting stronger."

She pressed down on two knuckles at once. "That must hurt," she said.

"It does. But you shouldn't have to be the only one dealing with pain."

She kissed the knuckles, lightly. "You and your crazy dad," she said. "What have I gotten myself into?"

VII. How You Might Feel

Claude came home late after another lousy night on the road. The fares had been fine, but the passengers had needled him. An extremely fat man flagged him down on Castor Avenue for a ride to Atlantic City. The guy smelled like smoked fish and he talked the whole way about his kidney surgery. "That's something you don't want, man," he kept saying. "That doctor stuck his stethoscope right up my dick. Man, that knocks the top off your skull."

For the trip back to Philadelphia, Claude's passenger was a thin, bitter gambler. "The bastards cleaned me out," was this guy's refrain. "I never had a chance. I remember when the Jersey shore was a place to bring your family. You remember that?"

Claude kept quiet and he was happy when he parked at home and he was happier to find Larry's message waiting for him. "Hope you're out having fun, Dad," the message said. "I was going to stop by in the morning. I want to talk about a few things. Call and let me know if it's a bad time."

Claude decided he should go right to sleep so he could wake up early and clean the apartment. He sat on the couch and thought about how long it would take, how the kitchen would require the most work. He poured himself some bourbon. The apartment had never looked so messy when Larry lived with him. Maybe in the morning he could run to the supermarket, buy some cleansers, a new mop, food for breakfast. Some large trash bags wouldn't hurt either. He poured more bourbon. He stretched out on his back, crossed his arms over his chest, and closed his eyes. He tried to remember the last time Larry had visited. It had been months. What did he want to talk about all of a sudden? It couldn't possibly be good.

The knocking was the next thing Claude heard. He got up from the couch, still wearing his blue jeans and T-shirt from the night before. He let Larry in, said, "I'll be right back," and then hurried into the bathroom. He called to his son through the door while he pissed. "I've fallen behind on my chores," he said.

"I can see that," Larry said.

Claude glanced at himself in the mirror, wet his hair, combed it, washed his face, brushed his teeth, pulled a sweatshirt over his T-shirt. "I planned to clean," he said. "I was going to cook breakfast. I was hoping you'd bring Jennifer."

"I want to talk a bit about Jennifer," Larry said.

Claude came out of the bathroom and sat back down on the couch. He plumped up the cushions around him. "Am I about to get scolded?"

Larry sat across from him, in the Barcalounger. He did not recline. "Dad," he said, "we love your coming by. But Jennifer's tired all the time. She's a little on edge—"

"Say no more. I understand."

"We still want you to come over. We're always happy to have you spend the night. We just need you to call first."

"Roger, dodger," Claude said. He wanted to say whatever would help them to move on. He would take what he could get. Accept what he knew he deserved. Gladly. But he didn't feel up to discussing it. "I could make some coffee," he said. "I think I've got orange juice."

Larry leaned forward. "Look, Dad, I'm not trying to give you a hard time. I just want everything to be all right between you and Jennifer. We've got years ahead of us—"

Claude wondered what Ellen would say at such a moment. She might tell him to keep calm. Maybe she would brush a hand through his thinning hair and encourage him to apologize. Say you're sorry, then stand up and rustle something out of the kitchen.

Larry kept talking. "Jennifer wanted me to be sure to thank you again for all the great stuff you've given us."

"I understand," Claude repeated. "You're coming through loud and clear." Then, before he could stop himself, he went on. "You shouldn't blame Jennifer, though. Say it yourself, like you said it before. 'I'm busy. It's not a good time. You messed up with one kid, you don't get another chance with mine.'"

"Dad, that's not what I'm saying."

Claude stood up. He folded and stacked the newspapers that were open on the coffee table. He stuffed a few crumpled napkins into his pocket. "You think you're ready to be a father? You don't know what the hell you're in for, son."

"I know I don't know," Larry said.

Claude walked into the kitchen to get the broom. When he started sweeping the floor, he saw his son stand up and come closer, still so goddamn handsome, still somehow unscathed, at least as far as he could see.

"Who could ever really be ready?" Larry asked.

Claude did not stop sweeping. "Not me," he said. "Not me. Okay? But you do the best you can."

Larry stepped into the middle of the kitchen and stood by the pile of dust Claude was gathering. "I'm not saying it the way I wanted, Dad."

Claude opened a cabinet and pulled out a dustpan. His head ached. His throat felt dry. He squatted down, gripping the broom lower. "Just tell me what you want me to do," he said. "I'll do it. Tell me what you want me to stop doing and I'll stop."

"All right, Dad," Larry said, and he squatted down, too. "I want you to give me that dustpan."

Claude handed it over. He wasn't sure if anything was better, but, together, he and Larry cleaned the whole apartment.

VIII. What May Concern You

A week later, Jennifer sat on the steps in front of her house. It was an early October Saturday, the sun bright in a clear sky, and it was the first weekend of her maternity leave, two weeks before her due date. The baby had dropped and she was having mild contractions more frequently. She looked up and down the street, reminding herself how pleased her parents would have been with her Manayunk investment—she had bought the small stone house with the money that passed from her father to her mother to her. They would have liked the fact that the house was too big for one person, sized for a family of three or four. The neighborhood was safe and it seemed to grow more popular—and more valuable—each year. First some antiques stores had moved in, then came galleries, restaurants, arts and crafts festivals, wine bars, bike races. While she sat there, a few bikers in colorful spandex pedaled by, training, maybe, getting their exercise before stopping on Main Street to grab a snazzy brunch.

Larry was off helping Shiroyama set up some sort of outdoor karate practice. "It's an advertisement," he'd said before he left, dressed in his new uniform—a pair of canvas pants, a heavy canvas top, and a white belt. A *gi*, he called it. She called it goofy. SCHOOL OF SHIROYAMA was sewn in large purple letters across the back of the top.

Her parents might have had some concerns about Larry. She could hear her father: A handyman? He's still a boy! What are his prospects? Her mother would have nodded in agreement, but then she would have looked on the bright side: He'll be good at fixing things. The imminent arrival of a grandchild would have soothed them both. Like her father-in-law, they would have quickly become overanxious about the baby, pushy, in their own way, reaching their hands out, too. She would have known how to deal with them, though.

The baby squirmed, interrupting her thoughts. It felt like she was being kneaded from inside. The baby wanted more space and Jennifer was sympathetic. She was waiting for Claude to pick her up so they could drive over and see Larry's practice, but she was tempted to skip it. She could tell Claude to go on without her and she could waddle down to Main Street by herself, order eggs benedict, read the paper while she sipped spearmint tea and ate a few chocolate-dipped biscotti.

The baby squirmed again and Jennifer looked down the street to see the white Taurus turning the corner. She stood up slowly.

As soon as Claude stepped out of the cab, he started doing some gibberish in the air with his arms. *"Hai-yah!"* he said. He tried a clumsy kick and almost knocked himself off his feet.

Jennifer kept her distance, walked past him, and climbed in carefully. She watched him slip in behind the wheel. When he reached across her, trying to help her buckle the seat belt, she waved his hands away.

"Look," he said. "I want you to know I understand."

Jennifer snapped the belt around her. "Understand what?"

"Larry and I had our long talk. I have no intention of being a burden, I want you to know that."

She didn't say anything. She was checking out the cab. The stopwatch dangled from the rearview mirror by a red string. The meter was off. Laminated licenses and certificates were taped to the dashboard, and in those official photographs, Claude looked at least ten years younger. How different he could have been, Jennifer thought. How different he *had* been. "Okay," she finally said. "Thanks."

They drove in silence toward Charles Peale Park where the practice was going to take place, near a playground, right beside Bethany Creek. Jennifer didn't enjoy watching Claude drive. It made her nervous, especially the way he rubbed at his eyes. On Roosevelt Expressway, he passed two SEPTA buses and each time he held his breath. She heard him exhale when they pulled in front.

"Did you ever date anyone after Ellen?" she asked.

"Sure," he said. "I went out on some dates." He smiled at her, clearly glad to be talking again. "I wasn't celibate. But I wasn't in great shape either. One woman I liked was a secretary at Thomas Edison High School. Larry wouldn't remember her. 'You're a real project,' she said to me. 'I'm looking for an easier time.' I told her I was looking for the same thing. But it went nowhere."

"You should keep trying."

"And I should stop drinking. Make some commitments to myself. Move on. I know."

It struck Jennifer as odd that Claude could sometimes seem younger than Larry. She saw it in his skittish gaze, a second of sulking, the shrug of his bony shoulders. She was learning more and more about feeling vulnerable. Soft. Exposed to so much possible harm. She stared at Claude, trying to predict where his vulnerability was leading him. "There's someone out there for you," she said, as convincingly as she could.

"Ellen said that, too. She tried to joke about it. Her friends who visited the hospital didn't know they were being judged.

Ellen tried to pick out a good mother for Larry, a good wife for me. None of her friends passed the test in the end. But she did like one of her nurses."

"Really?"

"Her name was Diane. There was nothing wrong with her. She wanted to help me get better." He exhaled, took a hand off the wheel, and rubbed at his eyes again. Then he went on. "I don't know," he said. "Some things only happen once. Other things happen over and over."

"Maybe you need a different job," Jennifer said. "Weren't you going to be something else?"

They turned onto Bethany Creek Boulevard, a few blocks from the park. There was a traffic light ahead and Claude hit the gas, trying to catch the green. He said something, but the engine drowned it out. Jennifer watched the speedometer. She breathed, closed her eyes and opened them. The cab kept accelerating. She glanced at Claude's foot and saw him flooring it.

"Slow down, Claude," she said.

His foot did not move. "Relax," he said. "We're clear. We'll make it."

The traffic light looked far away and it was already yellow. When they entered the intersection, two cars had to brake hard to stop in time. Jennifer started screaming at Claude to pull over and she kept screaming until he did.

Traffic moved past them and the cars that had skidded to a stop were gone. She looked across at Claude. He was leaning over the steering wheel, his forehead on his folded arms. She saw the ridges of his spine lift and fall. The two hearts inside her were racing. She climbed out of the cab and stood on the side of the road. Cars sped by, but she barely noticed. She saw the rough asphalt she was standing on. Small bits of rock stuck in tar. Pieces of broken glass. A paper cup tumbling.

Then Claude was in front of her, holding his hands up. "I'm sorry," he was saying. "Are you all right?"

She stepped farther away, from the asphalt to the grass. "How can I let you near my child? If you're going to be a god-damn, crazy—" She paused, gazed at the traffic light, watched it change. "Idiot," she said. "How?"

One of Claude's eyelids twitched. "I'll be better," he said.

"What if I can't believe that?" she said. Then she turned her back on him and started walking toward the park.

IX. Near the End and the Beginning

When it was time to start, there were eight other karate students in the park with Larry. He didn't know whether they had been invited or enlisted, but he did know they were all kids and he felt surrounded. He waited in vain for more adults to arrive. Then Shiroyama was leading the way to a space between the batting cage and the picnic area. "Three lines of three," Shiroyama said, and Larry stood in the back corner, looking over the group. They all seemed thin to him, still growing, their bodies struggling to keep up. Two of the kids must have come from elementary school. The rest looked like high-schoolers. Three of them had rolled in on skateboards. One was skin headed, another was as bearded as a mountain man. There was an Asian girl and a short, albino boy. The two grade school kids might have been speaking Russian. Larry thought he heard them say *Da* a few times.

Shiroyama's *gi* had a black belt striped at the ends with gold and he had tied a red bandanna around his head, like a kamikaze pilot. He led them through a long series of stretches, then basic warm-up exercises. He counted some off in English and some in Japanese. When he hit ten, Larry and the kids called out, "*Yoisha!*"

Once they were limber, Shiroyama jogged with them to Bethany Creek. On the way, Larry turned to the student beside him. It was the albino kid, his skin whiter than the canvas *gi*. Larry introduced himself and said, "So, what attracted you to karate?"

"I told Shiroyama I wanted to study Japanese culture," the kid said. "The truth is that people give me shit. I want to give some back. I'm Darryl."

Larry nodded. They crossed the bike path and clambered down to the creek's edge, where Shiroyama took off his sneakers and socks and began walking out into the water. Larry said to Darryl, "That water's got to be freezing. It'll ice over in a couple weeks."

Darryl already had his shoes off and was peeling off his socks. He didn't look up. "What are you," he said, "a pussy or something?"

Larry knelt down and undid his laces. Before he stepped into the water, he looked back for Jennifer and Claude. A bunch of people had gathered to watch, but Larry didn't see his wife or his father and he wondered where they were. He hoped they'd show up soon because he wanted them as witnesses. He also wanted that blanket from his father's trunk.

At first, the water seemed cold. After a minute, it was bone chilling, but the kids weren't complaining. Instead of cursing, they periodically shouted, "*Yoisha!*" Meanwhile, Shiroyama was striding ahead. When the water was an inch or two above his knees, he turned around, waiting for the lines to re-form. Then he started in with the punching drills. He counted them off, only in Japanese, and he counted much louder than he had on land, each number echoing from shore to shore.

Larry punched into the air and tried to stop his teeth from chattering. I'll leave when I can't feel my feet, he told himself. He peered over his shoulder at the growing crowd and saw no sign of Jennifer or Claude. Then he looked around at the kids. He expected some of the youngsters to drop out, dash blue lipped and shivering to their parents. But the kids were going at it. They were actually an excellent advertisement, rosy cheeked, their arms moving in time, their big white sleeves snapping in the breeze. They shouted together and Shiroyama shouted back.

Kicking drills began and Larry whipped his feet out of the water. The school of Shiroyama was suddenly full of dangerous Rockettes, splashing on the beat. Larry no longer felt so cold. He wondered what, in the years to come, he would watch his own child do. What bizarre activities? What unpredictable deeds? He couldn't wait.

"*Yoisha!*" he shouted.

CLAUDE WAS WALKING, following behind Jennifer as she plodded ahead on her unstable ankles. He wanted to explain what he had done, but he couldn't, not even to himself. He didn't know where to begin. Why bother to keep walking? She'd tell Larry the latest. Who could blame her? *Your crazy father tried to kill me. It's a miracle we aren't dead.* What could he say in his defense? Another failure. Another mistake. If I were my son, he thought, I'd tell me to get lost.

Explain, he told himself.

He had no trouble catching up to her. "Please wait," he said. "Just let me talk for a second."

She turned to face him, as close to him as she had been in the Taurus. "We're already late," she said. "So talk if you're going to talk."

He was tempted to reach across to her, but he dug his hands into his pockets. "You asked if I was going to be something else. Well, I *was*. And if I had everything to do over again—"

"It's not like you're out of time, Claude. You're not an old man."

"I'm not a strong man either," he said. "That's the thing. I used to think I was strong, but I'm not."

"I don't see what that has to do with speeding through a red light."

He didn't know exactly how to make that connection either, but he went on anyway. "Larry's strong. You may not know it, but he is. It's something that always amazed me. The way he manages—" He paused to clear his throat. "The way he manages to go on."

Jennifer didn't say anything, but Claude saw her shift her feet. She wasn't going away. He knew she might simply be uncomfortable, but it looked to him like she was settling in. Thinking. In any case, she was listening.

"The truth is there were days I resented his strength. I was grateful for it, too, but sometimes it pissed me off. I didn't understand how he couldn't have been touched by all that had gone wrong. I wanted him to know what it was like for me."

"So," Jennifer said, "if we got killed in a car crash, he'd know then? You'd teach him what it was like to lose a wife, a baby, and a father?"

"That's not what I'm saying," he said, shaking his head. But he could see how she was thinking and it sickened him. He had no idea how to convince her she was mistaken.

He watched as she crossed her arms above her belly. She looked away from him and away from the street, out over the grass, in the direction of the creek. "What am I supposed to say to you?" she asked. "What do you want from me?"

That he could answer. "Don't tell Larry about this. Say you'll give me another chance. That's all I want."

She kept gazing out at the creek and Claude waited. He remembered that New Hope afternoon by the Delaware River, years ago, his silly gift splashing into the water, his splashing after it, clear proof, even then, that everything was *not* under his control. What a stupid thing to have thought, let alone said! *One step at a time.* He had said that, too. A nice wish for another world, it turned out, but where he lived the steps blurred together. People lost their footing. They rushed and stumbled and fell.

And yet he hadn't done anything wrong back then, and he

didn't want to do anything wrong now. He'd gotten carried away in the car and he was sorry, but nothing like that would happen again. Ever. He felt certain. He *could* right himself. He *could* move forward. Improve.

He tried not to stare at Jennifer, but he couldn't help noticing the hard line of her mouth, the set of her jaw. She was strong, too, and he realized she might very well refuse him; he could easily imagine her saying, No. I'm sorry. If it were just me, then maybe, but it's not just me, so no. It was a punishment he could understand. She'd speak softly, a whisper, the words hard to hear above the rush of passing cars, and his knees would buckle.

Jennifer uncrossed her arms and massaged the back of her neck with one hand. "I'll think about it," she said. "Could you get the car? Please. I've had enough walking for now."

NOT LONG AFTER THAT, Jennifer and Claude were watching Larry, who was kicking and punching in Bethany Creek. Jennifer wondered over these two men in her life: My husband's playing in the water with a bunch of children and my father-in-law's worried about being told on.

She watched as the demonstration ended—the splashing stopped, the students bowed to their teacher, and the teacher bowed back. The baby inside her seemed inspired by all the activity. Kicking, punching, trying to stretch out. People around her were clapping, so she joined in, smiling as Larry came running to her, barefoot, his sneakers in one hand, his other hand waving. He actually looked dapper and brave in his goofy *gi*. "Did you see that?" he asked.

Claude spoke up. "We were a little late, son. It was my fault. I—"

Jennifer cut in. She wasn't yet sure what she would say about what had happened and she didn't want to be rushed into it. "We saw," she said. "You looked great." She paused to kiss his lips. "But it must have been cold. You're shivering."

Larry turned to his father. "I wouldn't mind grabbing the blanket from your trunk, Dad. Could I borrow the keys for a second?"

"I'll get it for you," Claude said. "You put something on your feet and talk to your wife."

He jogged off, leaving the two of them together. They walked to a picnic table, sat side by side on a bench, facing the creek, and while Larry slipped on his shoes and socks, Jennifer wrapped an arm around him, leaning close to share her warmth.

Larry looked up from his laces. "Were you two all right?"

Jennifer saw the teacher coming toward them, a small backpack slung over his shoulder. "I'll tell you about it later," she said.

Larry stood in time to say, "Honey, this is Kazuo Shiroyama, my client and teacher."

"It's nice to meet you at last," she said, and she started to stand.

"Please," Shiroyama said, "don't get up. The pleasure is mine. Your husband does excellent work. And he is also an excellent student."

Jennifer liked the way Larry blushed at Shiroyama's praise. "Let me ask you this," she said. "Will my husband's knuckles be okay?"

Shiroyama held his hands out in front of her face, turning them so she could see both sides. He held them still. They were not bruised or swollen, but they looked powerful. "His knuckles will be fine. Stronger than before." Then he pointed at her belly. "When does the little one arrive?"

"Soon," she said.

Shiroyama nodded. "I don't pay your husband enough. I will give your child free lessons, when the time comes, if you approve."

"You don't have to do that," Jennifer said. "Thanks for the offer, though. We'll see. Your school certainly seems to be off to a good start."

"It's too early to say. But I want to record some of this morning for my wife. I will do sparring exercises with a few of the younger students." He opened his backpack, pulled out a digital camera, and offered it to Larry. "Would you mind?"

Just then Claude, out of breath, returned with the blanket. From her place on the bench, Jennifer looked on as the three men tried to communicate. Larry took the blanket and draped it over his head, like a poncho. Shiroyama kept the camera by his side. "This is my father," Larry said, resting a hand on Claude's shoulder.

For a moment, Jennifer imagined the generations reversing, the father becoming more like the son, gaining surprising strength. She pictured her father-in-law not as a toddler and not as he was now, but as a young man, back before those cab license mug shots, back when he was a new husband about to become a parent, full of love, the world so open, promising more.

But she couldn't help seeing how Claude slouched, tired, unsure of himself, unsure of where he stood. He was looking at her, as if for a cue. All right, she thought, looking back at him. She'd try to believe in him and his desire to change. She'd try to forgive him, too, hope that he'd remember how to love without smothering. "Mr. Shiroyama would like some film of his kids," she said to him. "Why don't you give it a shot? The practice might come in handy."

Shiroyama held out the camera. "Please. I would be grateful."

"How does it work?" asked Claude.

"You can figure it out, Dad," Larry said. Then he sat back down beside Jennifer, wrapping her in the blanket, the soft blue fleece more than big enough for them both.

"Like this," Shiroyama said, showing Claude what to do.

Claude lifted the camera to his eye, sighted through it, held his finger above the red button.

"That's it," Shiroyama said. "Try it out on your family. You have quite a son. A lovely daughter-in-law. A grandchild on the way. You are a fortunate man."

Jennifer cupped her hand over her belly, searching for that new heartbeat fluttering beneath her palm. That extra pulse. Could the baby hear the young students laughing over by the creek? Could it hear Claude fiddling with the zoom, the sigh he made when he put his knee down on the grass, the sound of his voice when he said, "Okay, you two, I mean three, smile."

Jennifer wanted to smile for him, but she was thinking of all that had gone wrong and all that still might. Claude was so fragile and Larry was so young. She didn't feel afraid, but the responsibility was overwhelming, the burden and extent of it still growing, far larger than she ever could have expected. She inched even closer to Larry on the bench. He was no longer shivering. She caught the scent of gasoline, either from the creek water or the cab blanket. She didn't mind the smell. It felt good to be pressed up against her strong, solid husband, her open hand on his thigh.

"Come on," Claude said. "Smile."

"I'm trying," she said. Then she felt heat and a silver brightness push behind her eyes. Pressure bearing down. She leaned back and inhaled, counting the seconds. It hurt and it didn't hurt and she thought it might never stop. "I'm going to have a baby," she said.

Larry leaned over to kiss her cheek. "I know," he said.

She laughed at that, and smiled. "Soon," she said. "Maybe right now."

Larry jumped up and Claude quickly rose to his feet, handing the camera back to Shiroyama.

"Can I help?" Shiroyama asked.

"No, no," said Larry. "Thanks. We'll be all right."

Shiroyama stayed where he was, but he kept filming. It would be part of his gift for the family. He focused carefully, following the three of them as they walked away, side by side—father, mother, grandfather—moving off together as best they could.

Spring Garden

One Friday night, during dinner at Spring Garden Retirement Community, Victor Breslau picked a fight with a teenage waitress. Victor was seventy-six years old and he had a history of causing trouble. Once, he slapped a nurse so hard she banged into the wall behind her. More recently, he pinched a fellow resident and his nails drew blood. On this night, he wanted hotter coffee. He was shouting about it when he collapsed.

I had been working at Spring Garden for a few months as a resource assistant. I assessed the situation. I sent someone to phone for help. Then I started mouth-to-mouth. An orderly unbuttoned Victor's shirt and began pounding on his chest. I told a waiter to check for a pulse and keep track of the time. Victor's bristly white beard scraped against my face as I tried to breathe for him. His lips felt fat.

One of the residents shouted at me. "June! Save him!"

"He's all blue!" shouted another.

"No pulse," the waiter said, fingering one of Victor's thick wrists. "I can't find a pulse."

"Try the groin," I said.

I wondered what was taking the emergency unit so long. I wasn't a doctor, but I had almost gone to medical school, and I had some training. I knew we needed to shock him. We needed to get a breathing tube in. We needed to inject epinephrine into his veins. I inhaled and gave him all I had, again and again. A white scar ran down his chest from an old operation. He gasped once. His belly shook.

The orderly wasn't good at CPR. His elbows weren't locked and his hands were too high on Victor's chest. I tried to explain it to him, but he was wide eyed and panicking. I was glad to see Barry, my co-worker, rushing over. He pushed the orderly aside, knelt across from me, and started doing the compressions the right way. He counted them off: "One and two and three and four and five and *breathe!*"

The waiter had Victor's pants undone. "I think I'm getting a pulse now," he said.

Barry smiled. Then the paramedics dashed in with the defibrillator. "Stand clear," they said. We stepped back and they did everything they could. They intubated him. They shot him up with drugs. His whole body twitched each time they jolted him. But they could not resuscitate Victor Breslau. More than sixty of us watched him pass away.

Barry stood next to me and we were both sweating. I walked over to the waitress, who was still holding the coffeepot. She was the only one crying. She wiped her eyes with the back of her hand. I put my arm around her shoulder and said, "It's not your fault."

AFTER THAT, I wanted to drink and wash away the feel of Victor's lips. I wanted to go across the highway to Philadelphia's newest mall, where La Carreta had a late happy hour. I wanted to invite Barry. We'd unwind with a margarita or two. Maybe I'd make a play for him, maybe not. It was something I had been considering for a while, though I didn't like my chances. A typical evening together for us went like this: we'd drink, we'd chat, he'd leave, and then I'd walk across the mall to watch a movie. I was thirty-seven. Barry's gray-flecked mustache made him look older, but he was thirty-two, and he flirted more with the new nurses than with me. Still, the two of us shared good conversations. He was tough, he'd been through a lousy marriage, and he didn't know what to do next. So we had things in common. It wasn't hopeless.

One of the community's directors thanked us for our efforts. He shook Barry's hand and patted my back. Then he told us to give Victor's apartment a once-over before we clocked out. "One of our lawyers will come by in the morning," he said. "Let me know if that place needs to be cleaned up tonight."

On our way out of the dining room, Barry grabbed a handful of chocolate-chip cookies from the dessert table. "Well," he said, "that was awful."

His small glasses went nicely with his mustache. I also liked his thick fingers and strong back. He could have been a young sculptor from Barcelona, full of promise. He offered me one of the cookies and I bit into it.

"It wasn't pretty," I said.

"He never had a fucking chance."

We walked down empty, quiet hallways, toward Victor's. I imagined the discussions going on behind the closed doors we passed. A few residents would be grieving. As they mourned their latest loss, they'd also worry about their own fading futures. But most would be whispering their theories of what *really* happened. Some would say Victor's temper was a time bomb. They'd say such an end was inevitable. Others would say the death was the result of a mistake. They'd blame the waitress, the administration, the paramedics. Or they'd blame us. I turned to Barry. "Have you ever had to do that before?" I asked.

"Only on those practice dummies," he said. "Was this your first real one?"

"I did it in a hospital a few times, but I always had an ambu bag. I never had to use my mouth before."

"Yuck," Barry said. Then he smiled. "May he rest in peace and all that."

I opened the apartment door with my master key. The place was a mess. It looked as if Victor had been sleeping everywhere. Pillows and sheets were balled up on the sofa, the love seat, and the two easy chairs. Some of the pillows had pillowcases. Most did not. On the brown carpet, in front of the TV, he had spread a comforter and an electric blanket. There were empty jars and bottles all over, on the floor, on the glass coffee table—juice bottles, wine bottles, pickle jars. "What's it smell like in here?" Barry asked.

"You tell me."

"Microwaved cat food," he said.

"This is another part of the job I could do without."

"A combination of crushed ginkgo and Skin So Soft," Barry said. He picked up a pair of ten-pound dumbbells. "An iron pumper. He was training for the fight of his life."

"I still can't believe how hard he hit the floor."

Barry curled the dumbbells a few times and then set them down. "People get so sentimental about the elderly," he said. "They don't know how badly the old farts want to kick the shit out of you."

I looked at the veins in Barry's forearm. I looked at his lips. He looked away.

"I think we're done in here," he said. "I vote yes for house-keeping."

"Okay," I said. "I was going to stop by La Carreta on my way home. You?"

"Sounds good to me. A friend of mine's in town. We're meeting at the Hyatt by the mall. But not until later."

"Who's the friend?"

"Not really a friend, I guess. It's Blair, my ex."

We stepped out of the apartment and I locked the door behind us. Barry took a deep sniff of the hallway air. "Ahh," he said.

BARRY AND I had been hired around the same time and we'd met during orientation, sitting together while the orientation leaders stressed the importance of keeping the residents calm and content. We were told to smile, to hold back, to pile on politeness. Those sessions led the two of us to discover our nearby happy hour. Over cocktails, we usually loosened up and joked about working at Spring Garden.

"It's not a terminal position for us," Barry would say.

"We're lucky to be here at all. So many others are dying to get in."

"We shouldn't kid about it. It's a grave situation."

And so on.

During our first visit to La Carreta, I talked a little about my ex-husband, Raymond. I mentioned the restraining orders, the fight over the condo, and the other fights. "I know just how it is," Barry said. "The closer you are, the harder it is to get away."

It wasn't exactly what I meant. Still, I sensed he could be trusted, especially when he went on to describe his own ex. "Blair and I married young," he said, "and we became different people very quickly."

"I bet you thought you could grow together," I said.

"That's right," Barry said. "But you know what happens when you grow together."

I wanted to hear his version. "Tell me," I said.

Barry smiled. "You get twisted," he said.

La Carreta was the only dive in the mall, tucked away in a corner, directly across from a busy one-hour photo shop. Customers walked by, picking up photographs or dropping off film. They all seemed satisfied in the end, peering happily into their colorful envelopes. Barry and I watched from one of the restaurant's outermost tables, beneath a green, white, and red awning.

The two-for-one margaritas went down easily. We munched on free chips. "This woman—," Barry began.

I sipped my drink. "Go on," I said.

"Maybe I don't want to see her," he said. He swirled the lime green slush at the bottom of his glass. "Just because she's passing through town, just because she gives me a call—"

"You haven't seen her for a while, have you? Not since that wedding you went to, up in Vermont, right?"

Barry hunched forward, as if he had a secret. He took one end of his mustache between his thumb and forefinger. "She wanted me to know her new husband looked like me, at least around the eyes and nose," he said. "He wasn't at the wedding—too busy to make the trip, apparently—but she wanted me to meet him sometime, so I could see for myself. I told her a photo would be fine."

The waitress stopped by with our next two margaritas. "Everything all right here?" she asked. "One more round before happy hour ends?"

"We know what happens when happy hour ends," Barry said.

The waitress put the drinks on the table. "What?" she asked.

"It gets darker," he said. "And more expensive."

"Yes," I said to the waitress. "We'll have another."

A little later, we heard the shops closing up for the night. Metal gates banged into place and locked. Bag-laden stragglers shuffled toward the parking lot. "So," I said, "do you and Blair talk often?"

"I don't know about *often*. Never did meet her second husband, though. Proves that things can be avoided. We're drinking.

We could keep drinking. It's an option. I'm comfortable right here."

"Is the new husband with her?"

"They're divorced. Didn't even last ten months."

"What's she doing in Philadelphia? Did she say what she wanted?"

"What she wanted," Barry said. He glanced up at the awning. "Don't get me started. Look at this." He held his right hand above the table, palm down. The thick fingers trembled. "She wants to make me nervous. She wants me on edge."

I wrapped my two hands around his one, holding it still. "It's been a rough day," I reminded him.

He slowly pulled his hand back and I let go. "What the hell," he said. "You want to meet her? Why don't you come with me? We'll find out what kind of margaritas they make at the Hyatt, and you can see her for yourself."

I was interested, but I didn't think his offer was serious. I put my hands around my glass. "Are you afraid?" I asked.

"Of her?"

"Of being alone with her. Seeing your ex, after all this time. I guess it makes sense to be afraid."

"It's not fear. It's just nerves. I'm curious. Anxious, maybe." He paused and then went on. "Here's what it is," he said. "I don't want to do anything silly. If you come along, you can keep watch. If I start doing something stupid, kick me under the table. Tell me it's time to go. Say, 'Barry, we need to be leaving now.' Make up some kind of excuse."

"What if *I* do something stupid?"

"You? Like what?"

"I don't know. I could drink too much and then drink more, for instance. I had a different plan for this evening. It didn't involve new people."

"Or old people."

"That's true, too."

Barry slid his empty glass to the middle of the table. "It'll be perfect," he said. "Chug-a-lug."

As soon as we stepped into the hotel lobby, I knew which woman we were meeting. The tall blonde looked like a professional tennis player. She could have been Chris Evert's sister. She wore all black—stretch pants, blouse, and blazer. I'd never seen a picture of her, but Barry had told me she was a photographer based in Hollywood. She was talking to a man at the front desk and she had his full attention. "I want you to know how happy I've been with everything," she was saying.

"Blair," Barry said. He spoke her name as if it were an answer he'd been trying to remember for months.

The blonde kept right on talking while a short, black-haired woman stood up from a wing chair. The word that popped into my mind was *chunky*. This woman had heavy eyebrows and broad shoulders. She wasn't a tennis player. She was a wrestler. "Barry!" she said, opening her arms. "Come here."

It was a long, tight embrace. Blair pressed the side of her face into his chest. She was young, probably in her late twenties, but her neck had plenty of flesh. I wondered if she had always been that way or if the marriages had brought it on. Barry didn't seem to notice any change for the worse. His smile looked permanent. He was already being silly.

"Is this a new honey you haven't told me about?" Blair asked. She stepped back from Barry but kept a hand on his upper arm.

"No, no," he said. "This is June. We work together."

I shook the hand she held out. She squeezed hard. "It's nice to meet you," I said. "It really is. But you must both have a lot to discuss. I'll just leave you to it."

"Nonsense," Blair said. "We'll go to the lounge upstairs. We'll have a nice view. I'm sure you're here for a reason."

THE HORIZON LOUNGE was on the top floor, nineteen stories up, and it was much more elegant than La Carreta. The bar stools had high, padded backs, like small thrones. Through the enormous windows, we could see the Philadelphia skyline and, in the distance, the lights of the Walt Whitman Bridge, reaching across the Delaware River to New Jersey. Barry chose a table that faced Spring Garden, and he pointed to the other side of the highway, naming the community's various buildings for Blair—Liberty, Independence, Betsy Ross, the Franklin Hospital. We sat down in the plush chairs. There was a bowl of peanuts on the table. Before the hostess moved off, Blair ordered three Patróns.

"What's Patrón?" I asked.

"Tequila," Blair said.

"Just what we need," said Barry. He ate a few handfuls of peanuts. Then he wiped his fingers with a napkin.

A waiter put three shot glasses on the table. Blair looked at me. "June," she said, "how'd you wind up at a place like Spring Garden?"

I was busy being baffled by attraction. How'd she wind up with Barry? How'd I wind up chasing him? This is what it means to get older, I thought. You cease to understand. You work your dead-end job. Then, one day, you stop breathing.

I could see that Barry was waiting for me to answer. He didn't wait long. "She was going to be a doctor," he said.

"Was?" Blair asked.

"She's actually been admitted to medical school," Barry said.

Blair kept her blue-gray eyes on me. "Really? When will you start?"

"Barry's trying to embarrass me," I said. "The only school that accepted me was in Guam, and that was years ago. I'm not going there. I don't even know why I applied. At this point, I'd have to retake the MCAT."

"When will you do that?" she asked.

"That's what my ex would always ask me."

"And?"

I looked over my shoulder for our waiter. I wanted more than peanuts to eat. I also wanted to change the topic. When I turned back, she still had her eyes on me. "We went through some bad times about that," I said.

Blair was playful. "What? He felt threatened by the idea of a doctor-wife?"

I gave her a sample. "Some of our arguments went like this," I said. "I'm not ready. I've heard that before. I'll take it when I'm ready. Some people never get ready. What are you trying to tell me? I think it's clear. There are ways you could help. This is not about me helping or not helping."

I took a breath. Nobody said anything for a moment. I downed my shot of Patrón. Then I leaned back and crossed my legs.

"To exes," said Barry, raising his shot. He and Blair clinked their glasses before they drank.

The waiter stopped by. We returned to margaritas and ordered a few appetizers. More silence followed. "So," I said, "what did you two argue about?"

"Ha," said Barry. He kicked my ankle.

Blair didn't hesitate. "You remember what you used to tell me, Barry?" she asked. "It's one thing about you I'll never forget."

"There should be more than one thing," he said.

"Do you remember? The first time, it was an extremely hot day. That summer in England. We rented a rowboat on Windermere—"

Blair kept talking and I started in on my new drink. I'd never been overseas, but it was easy for me to picture the two of them together in the countryside, swim suited, fit, Barry working the oars. In every direction, they could see green hills, the trees still wet with rain from the morning's shower. They came upon an island. They pulled ashore. Even when they whispered, their voices echoed across the lake. They stripped down to skinny-dip in the cold water.

I knew it was sentimental romance crap, but that's where my imagination went. They would have been swimming while Raymond and I fought our fights. We shouted while they reached out for each other to keep warm. We should never have lasted all those years. I lost myself in the wrong questions: Would I be a mother? Would I be a doctor? Would I be either one?

Barry was insisting. "Come on, Blair. I give up. What did I used to say?"

Blair smiled. "You said that ever since you were a kid you knew you were destined to do something incredible. *Rare* was a word you were fond of. I found it very appealing."

"I said that?"

Blair turned to me, as if I had been in the conversation the whole time. "Did he ever give you that line, June?" she asked. "It's not a bad line."

"There's nothing incredible about what we do," I said.

"It seems rewarding to me," said Blair.

"Rewarding," Barry said. "Like looking after loud-mouth kids who happen to be absurdly fragile. You can't save any of them. The best you can do is give them a little longer—a year, a few months, a minute or two. It's a temporary detour for me. That's all."

"So destiny still awaits?" Blair asked.

"The door isn't shut," Barry said. "The door's open. I'm only thirty-two."

Blair smirked.

"Fuck you," Barry said to her, calmly. "I don't care if you believe me or not."

Blair chuckled and I knew I never wanted to confide in her. I figured she'd be safest if she was the subject. "What about you?" I asked her. "Barry tells me you take photographs."

"I'll give you the short version," she said. "After divorce number two, I went west. To Los Angeles. I met, I lunched, I cashed in. Now I do my art and I scout locations. I have some of my stuff with me, including a shot of my latest husband. The resemblance to Barry here is really remarkable."

When she reached into her bag and pulled out a small album, I excused myself. I had seen enough. I didn't need photographs. I walked off to find the bathroom and I imagined leaving from there. Maybe the whole evening had been a mistake. I didn't say good-bye, but I listened for the last words I'd hear from Blair. "And this is my house," she was saying. "There's a lot of space for just one person." I hurried past the bar and the throne chairs. Well-dressed men sat comfortably, nursing their drinks.

THE BATHROOM WAS as elegant as the lounge. I had it to myself, so I didn't rush. The light glared off the mirrors, the shiny floors, and the tiled walls. I fiddled with my bangs and fixed my part. The drinking hadn't been too hard on me. I was touching up my lipstick when the door opened and Blair walked in.

There was nowhere for me to go. She joined me at the mirror. We spoke to each other's reflection. "Here you are," she said. "That's a nice color. What is it?"

I finished what I was doing. "Rubysweet," I said.

"Can I try a little?" she asked.

I hesitated, but I wasn't going to say no, so I gave it to her.

She leaned closer to the mirror. She spoke to me as she worked. "You really look great. I couldn't believe it when Barry told me you were thirty-seven."

"Well, I've learned some defenses against old age on the job,"

I said. Blair was still chunky, but my skin would never be like hers again. "You're not even thirty yet, are you?" I asked.

"God, no. I've got time before that." She frowned then puckered at herself, checked her teeth, straightened up, and returned the lipstick. "Thanks," she said. "By the way, I was thinking we could all have a cup of coffee and then drop by Spring Garden. I'd love to see it."

I put the lipstick in my purse and turned on the water to wash my hands. "It's late," I said. "It will seem pretty empty."

She looked at herself from different angles. "Empty's fine with me," she said. "Do you know Eugène Atget? He loved empty. His cafés were empty, his courtyards were empty. The alleys, the streets, the balconies. Everything empty. His photographs showed how the world was a stranger to us all."

I needed to stop staring at her. I wasn't sure what she was talking about, but I liked listening to her. I reached for a paper towel. "I think Barry wants you back," I said.

Blair's laughter made that tiled, mirrored space feel like a circus fun house. "I don't know what I ever saw in him," she said. "That body, maybe. His eyes. But if you want him, he's yours." She turned from the mirror at last and she faced me. She stepped closer, her hands on her hips, still talking. "If you want me, we could discuss that."

I was watching her lips move. It was eerie. I backed away.

She laughed again. "I'll take that as a no," she said, smoothing her skirt. "But it's obvious you two are interested in each other. You should know this: little Barry responds well to commands."

Blair headed toward the stalls. She started to sing to herself.

I couldn't deny that she had a lovely voice, higher and softer than I expected.

WHEN I WALKED out of the bathroom, I saw a few people waiting for the elevator and, once again, I was tempted to leave. But leaving did not come easily. I glanced over to our table. Barry was sitting alone. Maybe he needed my help. There were three mugs in front of him, coffee seemed like a good idea, and I wanted to know what was going to happen. For better or worse, I was still interested. And I had promised to keep watch.

So the three of us made our way to Spring Garden. As we approached the main entrance, Blair stopped and took a small camera from her bag. Around us there were street lights, asphalt, curtained windows, a deserted lobby. The sky was overcast. Trucks rumbled along the highway. "You two keep going," she said. "This'll be a nice shot."

I heard the shutter clicking behind us. Then Blair caught up and we entered the building together. She kept her camera out while we strolled. "It's cavernous in here," she said. Barry told her about each room. Many of the common areas were dark. Blair took several pictures of the small library, with all the books, magazines, armchairs, ottomans, and the box of magnifying glasses. She also shot the game room, where there were pool tables and bridge tables and unfinished jigsaw puzzles. Her flash was hard on my eyes. She squatted, sat on the floor, climbed up onto a chair, getting the angles she wanted. She was full of energy, nowhere close to drunk.

Barry stayed by her side and they whispered to each other.

He seemed upset with her—his eyes narrowed, he stood straighter—but he let her pose him by a sofa. I could see that he photographed well.

I moved away from them. I walked up to the dining room where I was surprised to find the lights on and the door open. A silver-haired woman was sitting alone at a table near the kitchen. When I stepped closer, I recognized her as Milly Diamond, the resident who had been pinched by Victor Breslau. She still wore a white bandage on her arm. Her bony hands were folded in her lap and she was staring off at nothing. I sat next to her. "Milly," I said, "what are you doing in here so late?"

She turned to me. "You've been drinking, June. I would have done that too, but I'm not allowed. I kept thinking about Victor. I tried to sleep, but I couldn't stop seeing him and his blue face."

I touched her bandage with my fingertips. "He wasn't very nice to you," I said.

Milly sighed. "He wanted something from me."

"Maybe he didn't know what he wanted," I said. "Maybe he was just a bad man."

"You don't understand," she said. "He was hard of hearing. He was lonely. His arthritis was awful. He needed to have his way every now and then."

I didn't think she was going to cry, but her eyes seemed watery. I wondered what it would be like to see through them. "I did everything I could," I said.

She lifted a hand from her lap and patted my cheek. She smiled. "The coffee *was* cold," she said, wiping her eyes.

I looked over my shoulder and saw Barry and Blair coming

toward us. They were loud. Barry knew Milly and he introduced Blair. Blair was thrilled to meet a resident. "A person!"
she said. "And you have such a beautiful face!"

In no time, she was asking permission to take Milly's portrait. She lifted another camera out of her bag. I would have
saved Milly from that. I was prepared to help her to her room,
but she was enjoying the attention. She smiled and leaned forward when Blair brought out the photo album.

I stood up. "Barry and I need to check on something," I said.
"We'll be right back."

"Don't rush," Blair said, grinning.

Barry walked with me toward Victor's rooms. The fluorescent bulbs buzzed above us. I could also hear the low hum of
the community's power plant, somewhere underground.

This time, Victor's place reeked of pine cleanser. I closed the
door behind us and turned on the lights. Everything had been
straightened out. There were no bottles or blankets on the floor.
The furniture looked steam cleaned. It was as if they were expecting a new resident to move in first thing in the morning.

"It smells much better," Barry said. "Like a dying forest.
They did a fine job."

"Open a few windows," I said. "Let's get some fresh air in
here."

He stepped past me and slid two windows up. A breeze blew
in. He turned back to me. "Tell me this," I said, "how did you
ever wind up with that woman?"

"You don't like her?"

I imagined Blair helping Milly down the hallway, the two
of them coming to find us. Milly would tell Blair about Victor.

They'd enter the room and Blair would have her camera ready. She'd tell us where to stand. She'd go through drawers, throw open closets, searching for traces of Victor. A belt, a tie, a blanket, a bottle. She'd get a thrill out of arranging the three of us in a dead man's apartment. She'd laugh while she worked. Flash. Our faces shocked and wanting, preserved forever.

"Well?" Barry asked.

I could have told him that I admired how his ex set off sparks around her. I could have told him that I envied how, moment after moment, she made her surroundings seem more alive. But all I said to him was, "No, I don't like her."

Barry looked puzzled. He waited for me to say more. I let him wait.

I decided that if Blair actually did track us down, she'd probably stay hidden and shoot quietly. She wouldn't use a flash because she wouldn't want to stop me from moving closer to Barry. She'd understand I was doing what I needed to do. Despite what she'd said, I could tell that empty really wasn't fine with her, and I guess it wasn't fine with me either.

"Barry," I said, "I warned you I might do something stupid."

"What do you mean?"

I was beside him. "Are you afraid?" I asked. Then I took his face in my hands, my palms at his chin. I held him for a kiss. I tasted the whole night. I bit his lower lip.

"I want you to kiss me," I said.

Barry didn't move. I put one hand in his hair, the other on his neck. With my fingertips, I could feel his strong pulse. I switched off the lights. "Do it," I said. "Now."

Irreversible

I.

When Milly Diamond was seventy-four, she lost the sight in her right eye. She went on with her life. During the next seven years, she and her husband, Charlie, suffered the occasional minor setback, but the only major change was their address — they sold their suburban Philadelphia house and moved twenty minutes north to Spring Garden Retirement Community. Then, one Wednesday afternoon, Milly could not make out the words on the page of the mystery novel she was reading. The sensation was all too familiar — a black curtain dropping down. "It wasn't even a good book," she told the doctors. "I picked it off a shelf from somewhere to pass the time. I knew who did what after the first fifty pages. Still, I wanted to finish."

With great speed, and no physical pain, her left eye's optic nerve grew swollen, darkening her world.

"Irreversible," the doctors said.

Milly remembered back when, at sixty-five, she broke her hip. Her doctor told her she wouldn't bowl again. Told her she should give up her garden. Told her she would need a cane. Wrong three times, he was, and she loved to tell that story. How her tomatoes grew larger, how she took the cane he had given her and roasted it on the back porch gas grill, how she rolled a 227, twenty pins better than she had ever scored.

So, they told her she wouldn't see again. Four different doctors, two for eyes, one for nerves, and one for good measure, all agreeing with each other. "Sure, sure," she said. "We'll see if I see or if I don't. I can still tell what's red and I know where it's bright and where there are shadows."

The doctors assured her that it would grow increasingly difficult to distinguish between what she saw and what she imagined she saw.

Leaving the fourth doctor's office, Milly leaned on Charlie's arm and complained: "If these doctors don't have anything nice to say, they shouldn't say anything at all."

"Now, Milly," Charlie said. "They have to say something. It's their job."

"It's their job to make me better, and they're not doing that. That they always leave me to do on my own."

THROUGH ALL SIXTY-ONE years of their marriage, Milly had been the matriarch, without a doubt, leaving Charlie no chance to prepare for being in charge. The past had proven that she, like everyone else, was vulnerable, but Charlie was the one who had almost died, a veteran of a stroke and two open-heart surgeries. He was the one who had been flat on his back for weeks at a time, requiring so much care.

Sudden blindness could not change six decades. Milly still corrected him. She used her first few sightless days to learn how to knit by touch alone. She counted stitches and asked Charlie to check on each row, scolding him whenever there was a mistake. She talked at great length about the trips they had signed up to take and would take, no matter what he thought. They would fly to Florida, visit old friends, cruise through the Panama Canal. She'd be fine. "I'm not going to just sit here in the dark," she said.

CHARLIE HAD WORKED in construction for more than thirty-five years—as a laborer, a surveyor, and a foreman. After he retired, he spent hours imagining the design of the ideal retirement community. The basic model had to resist the predictable associations with last stops. And with waiting. Charlie envisioned a vacation resort. His final home would not resemble The End, it would be more like Club Med.

There would be bungalows, a big sauna, golf carts instead of ambulances, and a good-looking staff, all young, healthy, tan, and smiling. Keep the rooms simple to discourage indoor dwelling—get everyone out to the beach, the pool, the bright breakfast buffet, the lively evening entertainment. Of course people would still come and go, move in and out, but it wouldn't have to mean they had died. Think of it as a seasonal spot, with everyone traveling from time to time—Colorado for a winter of skiing, sunning in the Keys for the fall, north to Maine for the summer. If a couple never returned, it merely meant they had decided to spend their long vacation elsewhere.

He and Milly eventually chose Spring Garden, even though it fell short of his dream. Far short. Especially when the administrators ordered a red button for the wall of every living room in the complex. Two days after Milly went blind, all of the residents were suddenly required to press their new red buttons each morning. Charlie felt yet another unwanted responsibility settle onto his shoulders. He knew the terms and conditions of the lease he had signed. In certain instances—including repeated failure to check in on a daily basis—residents could be removed to the Hall for Assisted Living. No one ever showed him precise statistics about it, but the trend was clear: the Hall for Assisted Living was a corridor that slanted steeply down, sweeping its visitors off their feet, toward the graveyard.

"Rules and procedures fill this world," an administrator told him, "all designed with good health foremost in mind. To keep you well. To look out for your best interests. To make your time with us as comfortable and convenient as possible."

But Charlie was not the only one who saw it all as a slowly tightening squeeze. First they took your money, then they took your space and your freedom. In the end, they took whatever you happened to leave behind.

The red buttons came from the world of police, surveillance, and prisons. They did not belong in retirement communities and certainly not in vacation resorts. If I weren't so busy taking care of my wife, he told himself, I'd speak to these people. Give them what for.

ALTHOUGH SHE WOULDN'T admit it, after a week of blindness, nothing was getting easier for Milly. There were holes in the sweater she was making, and the sleeves were not the same size. Charlie kept asking her to meet with social workers or volunteers. "They'll understand what you're going through," he said. "They'll know about resources."

"Resources," she said. "You sound like a social worker yourself."

They were sitting at the kitchen table, eating the dinner Charlie had ordered in—a caesar salad, pasta primavera, lemon sorbet for dessert. Milly stabbed her fork into the salad bowl. The lettuce kept slipping off the tines.

"Let me help," Charlie said.

"I'll get it," she said, lifting another fork full of nothing to her mouth.

Charlie couldn't bear watching her. He put his face in his hands and sighed.

"Are you crying again?" Milly asked.

He shook his head, but she couldn't see. And he was crying.

"Go for a walk," she said. "Take a nap. I'm going to eat my dinner and then I'll watch TV for a while."

Charlie slid his chair closer to hers. He loaded up her fork a few times and she ate. He wiped her chin with his napkin. Then she took the fork back. "Really, honey," she said, her hand on his. "You need a break. I'll finish up here. It'll give me a chance to work on my technique. Go shoot a game of pool. Play chess. I'll be in front of the TV when you get home."

As usual, he did what she said. He walked up and down the long hallways, took the elevator to the recreation room, watched a few games of pool. Some people he didn't know asked him if he wanted to play. "No, thanks," he said. He kept strolling around the complex, wondering what it would be like never again to see the carpet, the wood railings along the wall, door after door, the bright watercolors, the windows, the slow-moving men and women. When he glanced at his watch, he was surprised to see that he had been away from the apartment for almost two hours. He rushed back.

Milly was sound asleep, curled up on the couch in her nightgown. The TV was blaring and he turned it off. He cleaned up the kitchen. At least all her food was gone. He went over and touched her shoulder. "You were asleep," he said. "Let's go to bed."

She sat up and switched the TV back on. "I want to watch a little more," she said. "I'll be there in a few minutes. Don't worry."

But you can't see! Charlie almost shouted. You can't watch anymore. He exhaled. "All right," he said. "I'll be waiting for you." And he kissed her twice on the forehead, once above each eye.

JUST AFTER THREE in the morning, Milly stood by the bed and shook Charlie awake. "Charlie!" she said.

"What is it?" he asked, sitting up. "Are you all right?"

"I just had a dream."

"A dream?"

"Let me tell you," she said, still standing, leaning against the bed. "We were going downstairs to eat with everyone again. I tried to get dressed myself, without any of your help. But when I stepped into the dining room, I was wearing only my bra and panties. Not even my newest. I tried to cover up. I stood there hugging myself, hoping I could somehow be invisible. I couldn't do a thing. You were gone and they all stared at me."

"I must have been there," Charlie said. "Where else would I be?"

"It was my dream," Milly answered, "and you weren't there. Someone I didn't know came up and gave me a blouse. She told me that if I sat at the table with the blouse on, no one would know how little I was wearing. I wasn't sure about that, but it was warmer to be half covered. Then I started to pull out my chair and, suddenly, I could see again."

"You could see?"

"It was like a bolt of lightning that stayed bright in the sky. There was a boom of thunder. The room shook. It seemed so real. Did you hear it?"

"I didn't hear a thing. It was your dream."

"I could see, but I didn't want to tell anyone. I didn't want to wake up and find out I was only dreaming. So I looked around, pretending I was still blind. I paid attention to everything in that dining room—the well-pressed napkins, the plain china, the shine of all the shoes. I stood up and walked slowly among the tables. People looked at my bare legs. They tried to hide their laughs with their hands. I was so happy I almost laughed myself."

"Then what happened?"

"I woke up. And I could still see. I could still see, Charlie. But when I turned the lights on, I was blind like before. I stepped into the dark bathroom, and I could see perfectly again."

"What are you saying to me, Milly?"

"Even now," she said, "in this darkness, I can see everything."

Milly climbed into bed beside her husband. "Am I dreaming?" he asked.

"I don't think so. This is just what's happening." And as she spoke, a strange, warm feeling circulated through her body, a pleasant heat spreading beneath the surface of her skin. She touched her husband. She moved her hands down his chest, tracing the line of scar tissue left by the incisions, resting her palms for a moment on his substantial stomach, then continuing to explore. His body responded.

"Oh my," said Milly.

"Milly," Charlie said. "Do you believe this?"

"Shhh," she said, moving her hands. "Don't say a thing."

THEY WENT BACK to see their primary physician, Dr. Sollman, and before they could get a word in edgewise he offered his assessment of the situation. He had followed Milly's and Charlie's health for years, and he was nearing sixty, so he felt he understood, in part, their longing and their desire to deny. "One-third of the entire cortex in the human brain is devoted to vision," he began. "That's a big chunk of brain, so when there's no vision left, things happen, nerves go on pulsing, and you might think you can see—flickers of color, bright light, shadow—but it's just that chunk of your brain playing tricks, searching for some new way to pass the time."

"Well," Milly said, "that's certainly very interesting, but the way it seems to me—"

"Let's just do a little eye test, and I'll show you what I mean."

Dr. Sollman hung a chart on the back of a closet door. "Read me some of those letters," he said. "Whichever ones you want."

"I can't."

"Of course you can't."

"It's too bright," Charlie said. "Turn off the lights and see what happens."

"She'll see better in the dark?"

"Just turn off the lights and find out for yourself. What can it hurt?"

The office grew dark and Milly rattled off letter after letter. She read aloud signs on the walls, all about heart disease and washing wounds and the possible meanings of dizziness. She read boxes of bandages, bottles of pills, prescription pads.

"Is this some kind of joke?" Dr. Sollman asked as he brought out a new eye chart. "Are you whispering to your wife, Charlie?"

There in the dark office, with her doctor standing right by her side, Milly read the entire new chart, without error.

"What else is happening to you?" Dr. Sollman asked.

"You have to promise to keep it a secret," she said.

"All right," he said. "I promise."

Milly told him almost everything. He made careful notes. He wanted to know exactly what pills she had been prescribed, when she took them, and in what combination. "You'll be coming back to see me, won't you?" he asked.

"Maybe we will and maybe we won't," she said. "You're always welcome to come looking for us."

II.

Mrs. Sarah Mandell, eating dinner in the Governor's Room dining area, ordered a large cranberry juice without ice and turned to her husband, Harold. "Another dinner," she said, "and no sign of Milly or Charlie anywhere."

Spring Garden contained several places for its residents to dine. The Governor's Room was the most formal. It was a fitting spot for Sarah and Harold. The two of them together looked like Americans who could live in Europe, even though they never had. They were tall, thin, and elegant, with striking faces and piercing eyes. They inhabited the retirement community as if they were elite expatriates, always ready to say that they really belonged elsewhere.

Harold did not go in for the keeping track of others. To do so would be, in a small way, to confirm the need for supervision. In fact, the red buttons, to his mind, were a punishment visited upon the residents because of their incessant gossip. Still, Harold did not close his ears. He called his wife a busybody. He downplayed everything she said, but he also paid careful attention when she spoke. "Did you check the menu for tonight?" he asked, trying to change the subject.

"That's more than a week now," Sarah said. "Do you think they got moved into the Hall? We should maybe stop by and see how they are."

"Milly went blind," Harold said. "You can't just go back to normal. They're still adjusting, probably. They don't want to go out yet. Let them get used to how different their lives are going to be from now on."

"Right," she said. "We should let them suffer in solitude, so they'll be better prepared for the future? How thoughtful."

"If you really need to know, you can call them. Talk to them on the phone."

"You can't be sure about the phone. They could be in bed unable to move, talking in their best voices. No, I want to see them, see how they look."

Sarah did not glance around the room as she spoke, but if she had, she might have been reminded of how misleading appearances could be. All of the residents looked as sharp as they possibly could—the men in jackets and ties, the women made up and bejeweled. And yet, at each table sat senior citizens with equipment bound to their aging bodies—canes, walkers, wheelchairs, carts with bottles of fluids, tubes threaded toward noses, through masks, directly into chests and stomachs. Longer inspection revealed bandages and scars, evidence of the internal work, the pacemakers, the prosthetic joints, the implanted valves, the thin, fragile skin too often opened and stitched shut.

"Let's have our dinner, Sarah," Harold said. "Here come Simon and Edna Goff. Let's ask them to join us. Don't forget to take your pills."

LATER THAT NIGHT, Harold drifted off in front of the TV. "I'm going to take a little walk," Sarah whispered toward his sleepy head, just so she could say she had told him. She strolled up the long hallway to the elevator, rode down one floor, and then walked to the Diamonds' apartment. It was nearly nine thirty, not late for her, but she knew that many people were asleep and had been asleep for hours, so she knocked quietly. "Milly, Milly," she said. "Are you in there? Charlie? It's me, Sarah." Then she knocked again, less quietly.

She did not like to be puzzled, but puzzled she was. She had known Milly and Charlie for years. In fact, Sarah had been the one who steered them toward Spring Garden, telling them all about the better sort of people, the distinguished atmosphere, the enduring friendships formed.

She backed up and squatted down a little, hoping to see light coming out from under the door. Before she could stand again, she heard the knob turn.

"Who is it?" Milly asked.

"It's me, Milly. Sarah Mandell. I didn't know what had become of you so I came by. I hope I didn't wake you. Harold didn't want to bother you. I had to wait for him to fall asleep before I could step out."

"Shhh," Milly said. "Shhh. Or you can't come in."

"I'm shushing. Absolutely."

THE APARTMENT RESEMBLED all of the other apartments in the building, Sarah's included. They walked through the small kitchen. There was a shelving unit along the living room wall, beige carpeting beneath their feet. They sat side by side on the couch.

"Can I talk to you?" Milly asked.

"Of course."

"No, I mean, can I talk to you and not have you talk to others? I can only talk to you if you can keep what I say to yourself. It's more important than anything."

"I promise. Absolutely. Except maybe for Harold."

"Harold's okay."

Sarah did not have a morbid imagination, but she glanced around and tried to sniff the air. She had heard stories of people who did not want to report, for various reasons, the death of their spouse. They'd keep the poor, decaying body in a locked room and tell everyone that their husband or wife was sound asleep. Eventually, someone would step in to take a whiff and a look.

"By the way, Milly," Sarah said. "Where's Charlie?"

"He's sleeping."

Sarah noticed the blinds drawn in the windows and across the balcony's sliding glass doors. "Is that why it's so dark in here?" she asked.

"Here's how it is," Milly began. Then she told her about the dream and what came after.

"Even now," Milly said, "in this darkness, I can see everything."

Sarah sat silent, much more puzzled than before.

"There's something else," Milly said.

"What else?"

"Charlie and I, we're getting younger. No one will believe it, but it's true."

Over breakfast, Sarah tried to explain it all to Harold. "She didn't look any younger to me," she said. "But the room was dark and she could see. She told me what I was wearing."

"Sarah, people don't get younger. She's gone blind and batty at once. It's very sad. No theory necessary. There but for the grace of God—"

"At first I thought something awful had happened to Charlie. I figured she had gone blind and he had collapsed under the strain of caring for her. She said he was sleeping. I began to wonder how long he had been dead. But I saw that he really was sleeping, snoring like an angry goose."

Looking over at the next table, Harold noticed three women fiddling with their hearing aids. "Shhh, Sarah, shhh. We can't talk about this here. It's probably already too late. Mrs. Siegel's at that table, isn't she? She's heard already. Everything you said, I'm sure, and more, as always."

As Harold had feared, Mrs. Vera Siegel was talking. She was the sort of woman who overadjusted her hearing aid and oiled the wheels of her wheelchair, just so she could approach undetected and learn the community's secrets. Naturally, after hearing Sarah talk about Milly's condition, Mrs. Siegel had to share the news—and, like all devoted gossips, she tended to exaggerate. Her version of Milly's "recovery" spread quickly, from ear to ear and floor to floor, gathering embellishments along the way, including: Milly had never gone blind, she'd simply cashed in on a special line in her insurance policy; Milly went gambling in Atlantic City and bet her sight on a blackjack game, lost, and then, two weeks later, won her vision back; in a deal with the devil, Milly agreed to see only in the dark, trading her soul for youth and diabolical sex. And then there was the most popular, predictable interpretation—both Milly and Charlie had contracted a fast-moving case of Alzheimer's, and they were slated to be confined for the rest of their days to the Hall for Assisted Living after a bit more paperwork was completed.

The residents wanted to speak with Milly and Charlie. Everyone wanted to prove or disprove what they had heard; they wanted to discover what they should take, why they were not chosen, how much money the treatment cost, and who the miracle doctor was. The anger, jealousy, and resentment that filled these demanding voices surprised Milly and Charlie, and they wondered what they should do to get on with their ever-improving lives.

When they stepped out of their apartment, they wore dark glasses and tried to act infirm. They walked arm in arm, with Charlie pretending to be the guide. Milly fluttered her free arm before her, feeling her way, holding back a smile as best she could.

Sarah Mandell wondered if it was just her imagination or if the Diamonds' faces were gradually growing less wrinkled. She sought more information, stopped by the room several times, but her knocks went unanswered.

The Spring Garden authorities heard stories and wanted a meeting. They cited the missed dinners and the fact that the Diamonds had failed to push the red button several days in a row.

A reporter from the local paper was said to be on her way.

III.

The night before the meeting they had been forced to schedule, Milly and Charlie made love, as they had been doing twice daily since they realized they once again could. They felt their bodies returning to them, more agile, and much, much younger. They turned the TV up to drown out the sounds they made.

Milly fell asleep listening to her husband's steady heartbeat, worrying ever so slightly not only about the imminent meeting but also about the potential tabloid headlines that would result if she somehow became pregnant. She and Charlie were changing at every turn. The irreversible reversed. Who knew what she would look like in nine months? Her sight back, her bones strong, her skin smooth.

The dream that followed these thoughts came as a relief. A man appeared before her, dressed all in white. At first, she could not make out the features of his face. His entire presence seemed blurry, a shimmering. "Not another doctor," she said.

"Not exactly," a calm, child's voice replied.

"Is this death?"

The figure in white smiled. Or, at least, she believed she saw a flash of white teeth. "Nah."

Day after day, questions had been nagging her. There was so much she wanted to know. What had she done to deserve this? Where was the choice made? Why was the darkness necessary? Where would they end up?

Just as she was about to start through her list, the figure said, "Questions can be so annoying, can't they?"

Milly nodded her head, wondering anew what to say. For a moment, she glanced around, trying to determine where she was. She had no idea. There was mist and nothing recognizable. Then the figure took a few steps forward. One of his legs was in a cast, and he was limping. There was also a cast on his left arm. Milly could see a gigantic wing rising up out of his right shoulder. He looked young and yet his hair was silver. Now she could see that he was indeed smiling. "Don't ask too many questions," he said. "Listen. The darkness is temporary. A period of transition."

Charlie appeared by her side, wrapping an arm around her waist. She was glad that this dream included him. "I've seen people die," he said. "Those people were not happy. They never felt younger than they were, not even for a minute."

"It's true," the figure told them. "That happens to some people. I have no explanation to offer you. Look at me." He turned his back toward them and Milly could see that he had only the one enormous wing. "I'm missing a wing," he went on. "I fall down whenever I try to fly. You wouldn't believe how many broken bones I've had. I don't know why. Did you say a special word, follow the right diet, or think the perfect thought—and now you get to grow younger? Nothing like that. Nothing I can make you understand. You went blind and now you can see, and now you can both go on."

"What will happen?" Milly asked.

"Go on and see."

THE DIAMONDS NEVER appeared for the meeting they had scheduled with the administrators. A search was conducted, phones rang, inquiries were made, but answers were not forthcoming. In the absence of answers, a simple story circulated. Milly fell from a stepladder, broke her leg, and moved briefly into the Hall for Assisted Living. Charlie went with her to keep her company and to avoid being all alone. He tried to reach his daughter, Barbara, and he tried to reach his grandson, Eric, but neither one returned his calls in time. For two days and two nights Charlie hoped to hear from them. He sat beside his blind and delirious wife, heartbroken. Predictable, inevitable complications followed and both Diamonds deteriorated with alarming speed. They were rushed to the emergency room, but nothing could be done.

There were, however, other stories. Sarah Mandell, for instance, told Harold that she saw Milly and Charlie, early in the morning, jumping into a little old sports car. "It looked rusty at first," she said. "But once they sat down, the whole body seemed to shine red, as if it had been freshly painted, right off the assembly line. The motor purred and roared and away they went."

Sarah told her husband this version of events as they dressed for yet another Governor's Room dinner. Before they walked out the door, she decided that she wanted to stay in. She went back into the bedroom and took off her clothes. She considered climbing into bed and wrapping the covers around her, but she wasn't cold.

"Let's go, Sarah," Harold called out to her.

She stayed where she was, the soles of her feet tingling against the carpet, her face flushed and warm. "I need to see you in here," she said.

Then she turned off the lights and waited.

Acknowledgments

With special thanks and ongoing appreciation for:

David Blake, John Gregory Brown, Carrie Brown, Christopher Castellani, Michelle Chalfoun, Doug Dorst, Elizabeth Graver, Tamara Guirado, Otis Haschemeyer, Marie Hayes, Adam Johnson, Eric Korsh, Jack Livings, Dan McCall, Malinda McCollum, James McConkey, Richard Newman, Katharine Noel, Ron Nyren, Julie Orringer, ZZ Packer, Angela Pneuman, Lysley Tenorio, and Richard Wurman

The Creative Writing Program at Boston University, especially Ralph Lombreglia, Allegra Goodman, and Leslie Epstein

The Wallace Stegner Fellowship Program at Stanford University, especially John L'Heureux, Elizabeth Tallent, and Tobias Wolff

The English Department and the New York State Writers Institute at the University at Albany, SUNY

Dorian Karchmar at the William Morris Agency

Antonia Fusco and everyone else at Algonquin

The lovely, wise, and utterly wonderful Elisa Albert.

Last but not least, my love and thanks to my amazing family, without whom nothing would be possible: my parents, William and Carol Schwarzschild; my uncle and aunt, Mark Merin and Cathleen Williams; my two brothers, Arthur and Jeffrey; and (especially and obviously) my *bubba* and *zayde,* Charles and Mildred Merin. Once again and always.

TELL ME SOMETHING

A Short Note from the Author

IN ONE WAY OR ANOTHER, I'm always writing for my bubba, the amazing family matriarch who inspired this collection and who is, in my mind, absolutely inseparable from Milly Diamond. I can still picture Bubba during her last years, sitting on her couch in Riddle Village Retirement Community, out on the edge of Philadelphia. She's become blind in her old age and, as usual, she holds her briefcase-sized tape player on her lap. Her eyes are closed and there are old-school puffy black headphones covering her ears. She's listening to yet another book on tape.

Before walking over to say hello, I can close my eyes, too, and it's easy for me to picture her at other times in her life. I'm fortunate that she started a family when she was young. She gave birth to my mother when she was twenty-two, and my mother followed her example, giving birth to me when she was twenty-three, so I began to know Bubba when she was still a vibrant young woman. It was Bubba who taught me to swim and bowl and play blackjack. Year after year, Bubba organized almost every major family event, and during every occasion, she told me stories about our history, our city, our friends, and our family.

Those stories grow out from one basic narrative. A young man flees the Russian army in the 1890s and comes to Philadelphia and walks the streets looking for work. He's been trained as a kosher butcher but the only job he can find is as a peddler. He meets a young woman who also fled Russia and they fall in love and marry and work and work and work and have five children, two boys and three girls, and Bubba is the youngest. These children become doctors and lawyers and teachers and secretaries and spread out all across the city. Many of the stories featured poverty and heartbreak and sickness and bankruptcy, but in the end they were stories of triumph, of adversity overcome.

I want to say that Bubba's own story line was also triumphant, and on most levels it was — she created and nurtured a growing family, and nothing was ever more important to her than that. But over the years her body failed her. Still, she was stubborn to the end, determined to do as much as she could. To give just one example, in her late seventies, she wanted to go white-water rafting in Colorado, even though by then her left eye had already stopped working. She couldn't understand our hesitation. "I'll be fine," she said. "You don't have to worry about me." We almost believed her — she was always very convincing — but that was one of the rare times she didn't get her way.

Back at Riddle Village, I walk over to where she's sitting on the couch. I touch her hand, sit beside her, kiss her cheek, and she opens her sightless hazel eyes. She takes off the headphones and moves the tape player onto the coffee table. Then she starts to talk. Her voice has become raspy and she wheezes a little with every breath, a constant reminder that she's the last of her siblings still alive. Sometimes it sounds to me as if her brothers and sisters are all trying to speak through her. Maybe those voices fighting for space inside her are part of what makes it more difficult for her to breathe. In any case, she opens the conversation the same way she always does. "Tell me something," she says.

I can't refuse. I tell her everything I can, about my life, my work, my girlfriend.

But she wants more. For her—forever our family gardener, baker, canner, chef, seamstress, pianist, bowler, swimmer, cyclist, knitter, mah-jongg maven, school district secretary, matriarch, and Bubba—actions have always spoken much louder than words. "When will the book be finished?" she asks. "And where are my great-grandchildren?"

I assure her that I'm working on everything as best I can. I tell her it's my job to give her something to look forward to. Then I mention a story that's giving me trouble. There's always a story giving me trouble.

She leans forward, rests a hand on my knee, and says, "I bet the characters will take over. They'll tell you what to put down on the page. At least that's what I've heard from other writers. Hasn't that happened for you yet?"

"No," I answer, "not yet."

But then, later, after I leave, I eventually return to my desk and I can feel Bubba's voice pushing my writing forward. She's there, by my side, whispering and wheezing words of encouragement. And that encouragement never seems to stop. Bubba died five years ago while she was traveling in California, but I swear I can hear her voice whenever I sit down in my study. "Tell me something," she says.

I still can't refuse. I tell her everything.

"When will the next book be finished?" she wants to know, as usual.

"It's finally done," I say. "And, guess what, it's dedicated to you."

"That's nice," she says. "But where are my great-grandchildren?"

"I'm working on that," I promise.

JENNIFER MAY

EDWARD SCHWARZSCHILD is the author of *Responsible Men,* a *San Francisco Chronicle* Best Book of the Year, a Book Sense Notable Pick, and finalist for both the Rome Prize from the American Academy of Arts and Letters and the Samuel Goldberg and Sons Foundation Prize for Jewish Fiction. His work has appeared in the *Believer, Moment, jewcy.com, StoryQuarterly,* and the *Yale Journal of Criticism,* among other publications. He divides his time between Brooklyn and upstate New York, where he is an associate professor at the University at Albany, SUNY, and a fellow at the New York State Writers Institute.

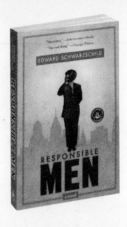

- A *San Francisco Chronicle* Best Book of the Year
- A *Kirkus Reviews* Great Book Group Pick
- A Book Sense Notable Pick

—◆—

"A moving, impressive debut. . . . Marvelous."
—Ha Jin, author of *War Trash* and *Waiting*

"Schwarzschild tells this modern morality tale of redemption and forgiveness with measured confidence." — *San Francisco Chronicle*

"This novel is the real thing." — *Chicago Tribune*

"The suspense, humor and human connections that Schwarzschild concocts makes this original work stand out." — *The Jewish Week*

"A compassionately and deftly told story."
—William Kennedy, author of *Ironweed* and *Roscoe*

"Early in Schwarzschild's marvelous debut novel, Max Wolinsky issues a warning: 'Let the buyer beware.' But it's impossible to avoid falling for Max, even if he is a small-time con. . . . That's how appealingly the author has designed our hero, not to mention his cohorts." —*Entertainment Weekly*